Beth touched her lips. Had Jake really kissed her?

The butterflies still in her stomach told her he had. Passionately. Hard. But she reminded herself that nothing more could come of it.

They were from two different worlds. And besides, she didn't want to get involved with anyone, especially not Jake Dixon. He was the type of man she could easily lose her heart to. And she didn't want a man in her life. Not now.

She was happy living with her son, just the two of them. And Jake Dixon drank. She remembered seeing him drinking a beer last night. No *way* was she going to let another man like that into her life.

No way on earth.

Then *why* had she accepted his invitation to go out tonight?

Dear Reader,

Well, we hope your New Year's resolutions included reading some fabulous new books—because we can provide the reading material! We begin with *Stranded with the Groom* by Christine Rimmer, part of our new MONTANA MAVERICKS: GOLD RUSH GROOMS miniseries. When a staged wedding reenactment turns into the real thing, can the actual honeymoon be far behind? Tune in next month for the next installment in this exciting new continuity.

Victoria Pade concludes her NORTHBRIDGE NUPTIALS miniseries with *Having the Bachelor's Baby,* in which a woman trying to push aside memories of her one night of passion with the town's former bad boy finds herself left with one little reminder of that encounter—she's pregnant with his child. Judy Duarte begins her new miniseries, BAYSIDE BACHELORS, with *Hailey's Hero,* featuring a cautious woman who finds herself losing her heart to a rugged rebel who might break it.... THE HATHAWAYS OF MORGAN CREEK by Patricia Kay continues with *His Best Friend,* in which a woman is torn between two men—the one she really wants, and the one to whom he owes his life. Mary J. Forbes's sophomore Special Edition is *A Father, Again,* featuring a grown-up reunion between a single mother and her teenaged crush. And a disabled child, an exhausted mother and a down-but-not-out rodeo hero all come together in a big way, in Christine Wenger's debut novel, *The Cowboy Way.*

So enjoy, and come back next month for six compelling new novels, from Silhouette Special Edition.

Happy New Year!

Gail Chasan
Senior Editor
Silhouette Special Edition

Please address questions and book requests to:
Silhouette Reader Service
U.S.: 3010 Walden Ave., P.O. Box 1325, Buffalo, NY 14269
Canadian: P.O. Box 609, Fort Erie, Ont. L2A 5X3

The Cowboy Way

CHRISTINE WENGER

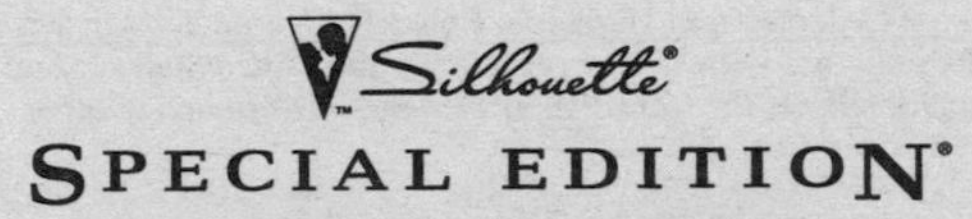

Published by Silhouette Books
America's Publisher of Contemporary Romance

There are so many wonderful friends I'd like to thank for making my dream come true. The Packeteers have been with me from the beginning, and I thank them from the bottom of my heart. The Sisters of the Lake were there when I needed a boost.

Throughout the years, Pat Kay, Carla Neggers and Maggie Shayne gave graciously of their time and knowledge and made me a better writer.

And to Amber Schalk who taught me never to give up.
I think of you often, Amberoni.

This one's for you, ladies—fabulous writers
and fabulous friends. I love you all!

SILHOUETTE BOOKS

ISBN 0-373-24662-5

THE COWBOY WAY

This edition published by arrangement with Harlequin Books S.A.

Visit Silhouette Books at www.eHarlequin.com

Printed in U.S.A.

Books by Christine Wenger

Silhouette Special Edition

The Cowboy Way #1662

CHRISTINE WENGER

has worked in the criminal justice field for more years than she cares to remember. She has a dual master's degree in probation and parole studies and sociology from Fordham University, but the knowledge gained from such studies certainly has not prepared her for what she loves to do most—write romance!

A native central New Yorker, she enjoys watching professional bull riding and rodeo with her favorite cowboy, her husband, Jim.

GOLD BUCKLE RANCH
MOUNTAIN SPRINGS, WYOMING

CONGRATULATIONS TO
BETH CONROY AND KEVIN CONROY!

Dear Kevin,

We are happy to inform you that your essay—about how your mother needs a vacation and how you'd like to participate in Wheelchair Rodeo—has touched our hearts. Therefore, you are both invited to spend a free week at Gold Buckle Ranch located in beautiful Mountain Springs, Wyoming, during the second week of July.

Your mother will find that our facilities promote rest and relaxation. Troubles are soon forgotten at the Gold Buckle Ranch, as one spends sunshine-filled days walking among the wildflowers on any one of our beautiful trails.

Kevin, as you know, Wheelchair Rodeo is the idea of our son, world champion bull rider Jake Dixon. In your application, you stated that Jake has been your hero since before your accident. Therefore, you'll be happy to know that Jake will be personally helping you pick out a horse and teaching you to ride. He'll also be happy to help you mom get used to ranch living.

We guarantee that you'll both have a wonderful time at the Gold Buckle Ranch!

Very truly yours,

Dex & Emily Dixon

Chapter One

Beth Conroy looked outside and saw her son parked in his usual spot at the end of the driveway, waiting for the mail to be delivered.

Every afternoon since Kevin had entered the Gold Buckle Ranch contest, he had wheeled himself down to the mailbox at the foot of the driveway at three-thirty sharp in the hope that a letter would come from Wyoming, informing him that he was a winner.

He had on his black cowboy hat as usual, the one she got him for Christmas, and he wore a big silver belt buckle, jeans and a long-sleeved western shirt. Not unusual for Lizard Rock, Arizona—most everyone dressed in the western style, but once in a while other kids wore shorts and a T-shirt.

Not Kevin.

Every article of clothing on him, except maybe his

underwear, was from the "Jake Dixon Collection." If something didn't sport the name of Jake, his favorite bull rider, Kevin didn't wear it.

Waiting, hoping, looking so alone, he craned his neck toward every car or truck that came down the street. "Today it'll come," he'd told her earlier, total trust shining in his eyes.

Five minutes later, when the white truck with the blue eagle on the side turned the corner, she saw him wave his fist in the air.

"All right! Cool!" he shouted.

To a ten year old, it must have seemed to take forever for Mrs. Owens, the mail carrier, to reach their mailbox. Beth stepped closer to the screen door so she could hear the conversation.

"Hi, Kevin," Mrs. Owens said. She leafed through a handful of mail and smiled. "It's here. Gold Buckle Ranch, Mountain Springs, Wyoming."

"Yesss!"

Beth held her breath. It would mean so much to Kevin if he won the contest, but realistically the odds were against him. She didn't want him hurt any more.

Mrs. Owens reached over the side of the truck and handed him the letter. He stared at it. Beth knew that because Kevin wanted it so much, it had never occurred to him that he wouldn't win the contest.

It had never occurred to her that he would.

He smoothed out the envelope. Win or lose, he'd want to save it along with the letter and glue them into his Jake Dixon scrapbook or hang it on his bulletin board, another shrine to the popular cowboy.

"Would you like to take the rest of the mail?" asked Mrs. Owens.

"Sure." He stuffed everything into the canvas bag that hung from the side of his wheelchair. "Thanks, Miss Owens."

"Hope you won, Kevin."

"I did!"

As fast as his hands could spin the wheels, he tore up the driveway and the ramp to the rental office. "Mom! It's here!"

Beth opened the door for him and stepped back, laughing. "Slow down before you run over my toes."

He stopped in front of her. "Guess what?"

"Something important come in the mail?"

With fumbling fingers, he pulled the envelope out of his canvas bag and held it up to her.

"I hope it's good news, sweetie."

He let out a puff of air, carefully opened the envelope and unfolded the letter.

When Beth heard his resounding "Yee-haw!" and watched him turn his chair in a complete circle, she knew that he'd won the Gold Buckle Ranch contest. Her heart filled with joy to see him so happy.

"Mom!" he yelled. "This is so cool!"

"We won the lottery?"

"Better than that."

"What could be better?" She knew the answer to her own question. Seeing her son walk again would be better than all the money in the world.

"Going to the Gold Buckle Ranch in Wyoming and being in Wheelchair Rodeo." With a big grin, he handed her the letter. "I won the contest, Mom. I mean, you won. We *both* won!"

Beth skimmed the letter and contemplated several problems. Sneaking a peek at her son's bright eyes and big, wide grin, she couldn't tell him that the plane trip from Lizard Rock, Arizona to Mountain Springs, Wyoming would wipe out her meager savings. She wasn't entitled to a paid vacation yet, either. Any time off would be without pay. She had stacks of bills. Kevin was probably going to need another operation. There was that specialist in Boston and…and…

She took a deep breath. She knew how much going to the Gold Buckle Ranch meant to Kevin. She'd watched him sweat over his entry. She'd helped him look up words in the dictionary, but he wouldn't let her read the entire essay.

"What exactly did you write?" she asked.

"I told them why you needed a vacation in a hundred words or less. It only took me seventy-one words, and that's counting the small ones."

She bit back a smile. "And why do I need a vacation?"

"'Cuz, Mom…'cuz you worry about me. And Dad died. And we had to move to this crummy place. And 'cuz you have to work all the time."

His smile faded as his forehead wrinkled with worry lines no ten year old should have. It had been a tough two years for both of them. After the accident, Kevin had undergone four operations and thousands of hours of physical therapy. It was way too much for a little boy to handle. She could barely handle it herself. She had hoped and prayed that his last operation would be a success, but Kevin showed no sign of improving. The surgeons were puzzled. She was devastated.

She had to save enough money to take him to Boston, to see the specialist, but now this…

Beth walked to his side. She crouched down and ran her fingers through his soft, shiny hair that was so much like Brad's had been.

"Sweetie, I'm okay. We had to make some changes, like selling the house and moving here, but we're doing all right. Aren't we? There's a pool…and you like your school." She faltered. There had to be more reasons. "Aren't we doing okay?"

Kevin's knuckles were white as he gripped the arms of his wheelchair. "We're doing okay, Mom. But you need a vacation."

"And maybe you do, too, huh?"

He smiled. The spark in his eyes was back. "I'm going to be in Wheelchair Rodeo. Jake Dixon and Clint Scully and Joe Watley and tons more cowboys do Wheelchair Rodeo every year at the Gold Buckle. There's a campout and trail rides—on horses, Mom. On *horses!*"

He paused for a quick breath. "And the cowboys teach us how to rope, too. I wish they were real steers, but they're plastic steer-heads stuck in a block of hay. I'll show you the picture. And then there's this big, huge rodeo—a *real* rodeo. And the cowboys come from all over. All the cowboys I watch on TV will be there, but especially Jake Dixon. The Gold Buckle Ranch is Jake's ranch, Mom, and I can meet him, and talk to him, and he'll teach me to ride. And we'll be staying for a week and…"

Beth was mentally adding up expenses, but she let him ramble on. She loved it when he was happy and excited and acting like a ten year old again. She'd heard nothing but "Jake Dixon this" and "Jake Dixon that" since Kevin was six and had first shaken Jake's hand at the *Fiesta de los Vaqueros,* Tucson's annual rodeo.

Jake had won the bull riding competition that night and had stayed in the arena to sign autographs. Beth had waited in line with Kevin for over an hour, and Jake had autographed Kevin's program and given him a red bandana. Then Jake had taken the time to talk to him, making the little boy feel special. Ever since, Kevin had thought of Jake as his special hero, a larger-than-life figure who did much cooler things than any baseball or football star.

Jake Dixon had paid him more attention in those five minutes than Kevin's own father had in a week.

After that, the rodeo became an annual event and Kevin got three more autographed programs, had three more conversations with Jake and got three more bandanas.

Then the accident happened, and it seemed that whenever the Tucson Rodeo was scheduled, so was another operation.

During one of his hospital stays, Kevin had seen Jake being interviewed on TV. On a whim, Beth had e-mailed Jake's fan club, explained the situation and asked if they'd send an autographed picture of Jake to Kevin at the hospital. They did just that. They also sent him a western shirt, the one he had on today.

"Be tough, Kevin. Cowboy up!" Jake had written with a black felt pen. Kevin had insisted on framing it,

and Beth had found the perfect frame in the hospital's gift shop—silver with bulls on each corner.

With that picture and autograph, Jake Dixon did more to help Kevin heal than all the doctors could. Again this stranger had come through when her son needed a hero the most.

If somehow she could arrange a week off, she could only pray that Jake would live up to her son's expectations. She herself had no expectations as far as men were concerned, but if Jake proved undeserving of Kevin's adoration, he'd answer to her.

She ruffled Kevin's hair and stood. She had made her decision. "Well, I guess we'd better go to the Gold Buckle Ranch and meet Jake Dixon."

"Really?"

"Really."

She reached out to hug him, and for a second, she thought he was going to stand. Tears stung her eyes as she gathered him close to her. If she had to, she would sell her soul to get the time off to give Kevin this trip to Wyoming.

"Thanks for winning the trip for us, sweetie," she said, hoping she sounded convincing. "We're going to have a great time."

Checking the clock on the wall, she saw that it was almost time for Kevin's water therapy. She had two rent checks to collect and a phone call to make before she could close the office for the day and watch the therapist work with Kevin.

"You'd best get your bathing suit on. Sam will be here in a half hour for your exercises. I'll be in to help you change."

"I can do it."

"But—"

He was off in a flash of chrome and denim, wheeling up the ramp that led to their small apartment in the back of the office.

She felt a pang of sadness when she remembered that Kevin had called their apartment "crummy." It was crummy compared to where they used to live—a brand-new, four-thousand-square-foot house in the Catalina Mountains crowning Tucson. There they'd had wide-open spaces and room to run. It was a perfect spot for a kid growing up.

In contrast, their apartment complex was crowded with cars, concrete and cul-de-sacs.

Their life had been fairly good before the accident. Before her husband Brad had picked up eight-year-old Kevin from his friend's house and crashed into the concrete pilings of a bridge.

That was two years ago, yet she always felt physically sick whenever she thought of that day, that minute, that second that had forever changed her life and Kevin's. She would live with the guilt forever.

She should have known that Brad had started drinking again. She should have known....

She had been driving home from the grocery store that day when she saw Brad's cherry-red convertible crushed against a wall of concrete. She'd jumped out of her car and run as fast as she could toward the accident, but the police had caught her and pulled her away. Helpless, she'd watched and waited, crying hysterically, as police and firemen pried the mangled metal of the car away from Kevin to get him out.

She was screaming his name so loudly that Kevin heard her. He lifted his hand and waved. She knew then in her mother's heart that he was going to live. They'd let her hold his hand until they sedated him and got him ready for the ambulance.

As Kevin dozed, a kind policeman took her over to see Brad. He was already dead, lying in a ditch along the side of the road. A bright blue plastic sheet covered his body.

She knelt down, lifted the sheet and saw her husband, finally at peace.

Alcohol had claimed Brad, but it wouldn't take her little boy, not while she had a breath left in her. She'd kissed Brad's forehead for the man he used to be, taking one last look and remembering happier times. She'd let her tears fall, and when they dropped onto his face, she brushed them off and then covered him.

"Your husband didn't have his seat belt on, but your boy did. That saved him," said the cop.

She got into the ambulance with Kevin, and didn't let go of his hand until they wheeled him into the operating room.

Beth shook away the memory and blinked back her tears. Relaxing her clenched fists, she poured herself a drink of water from the cooler and drank it down. She had to concentrate on business right now, so she would be able to watch Kevin's progress with Sam. Then she'd make dinner, read the information from the Gold Buckle Ranch, and enjoy her son's company for the rest of the evening.

Kevin was her whole life, and to make things up to

him, she would give him the world if she could. But since she couldn't, the least she could do was give him Jake Dixon.

Jake signed a dozen autographs in front of the baggage claim area at the little airport outside Mountain Springs. When he was on top of the Professional Bull Riders point standings, hundreds of people used to crowd around him. He'd loved every minute of it.

A dozen fans would have to do, since these days he was ranked number thirty-nine out of forty-five pro bull riders. He was just hanging on to the tour by his ragged fingernails.

Jake checked his watch for the hundredth time. Instead of being cooped up in the dinky little airport, he would rather be mending fences or working with the new mustang he'd just bought from Joe Watley, a stock contractor.

Better yet, he'd rather be riding bulls on the Professional Bull Riders tour and working on pumping up his ranking.

But nothing was scheduled for the month of July on the tour, so he'd take care of business at the ranch and work on organizing the Jake Dixon Gold Buckle Bull Riders Challenge and Wheelchair Rodeo like he'd done for the past two years.

From what he could tell so far, they were going to have a bigger crowd than ever for the Gold Buckle Challenge. Area hotels were booked solid and so were area campgrounds. This meant a nice boost to the local economy and an even bigger boost for the Gold Buckle Ranch.

He really loved organizing and running Wheelchair

Rodeo for the kids. At least he was doing something that made him feel needed instead of angry and frustrated, the way he usually did these days.

He walked the short distance to the one waiting room, his back and right leg screaming for mercy. He checked the clock and sat down on a yellow plastic chair that was welded to three other yellow plastic chairs. Stretching his legs in front of him, he waited. Fifteen minutes later, people began filing into the waiting room.

He watched and waited, but others picked up all the passengers. Soon he was alone.

Shifting in his chair, he pulled the piece of paper his mother had given him from the back pocket of his jeans and checked it against the sign to the left of the door. Flight 1843. This was the correct gate.

Jake looked around for someone to ask about Beth and Kevin Conroy and when they might be arriving.

"Mom, it's him! It's Jake Dixon! He's really here! He's here!"

Jake couldn't help but grin as he found the source of the noise—a cute-as-hell, freckle-faced boy in a wheelchair.

The beautiful blonde who pushed the boy stifled a yawn. It must have been a long flight.

The boy wiggled in his wheelchair and waved his hands in the air. "Jake! Jake! Remember me, Kevin Conroy? And this is my mom."

Jake tipped his hat to her. Immediately he was drawn to her eyes. They were as green as the new grass that sprouted along the Silver River in the springtime.

"Wyoming will never be the same, now that your

biggest fan has landed, Mr. Dixon." She held out her hand. "I'm Beth Conroy. As you now know, this is Kevin. You've met him at the Tucson Rodeo a couple of times."

He shook her hand, glad for the heads-up. He'd met so many kids over the years, he couldn't remember them all.

"Sure. Howdy, Kevin. Good to see you again." He hunkered down and shook Kevin's hand. The boy had a nice strong grip, and his eyes were round with excitement.

What a darn shame that he was in a wheelchair. What a darn shame that any child in this world had to be disabled, handicapped, impaired—whatever the latest politically correct term was. It always twisted his gut. That was one of the reasons he'd started Wheelchair Rodeo—to give kids like Kevin the chance to be like other kids.

"Are you ready for Wheelchair Rodeo, Kevin?" Jake asked.

"Yes. I can't wait. It's going to be awesome!"

"We have a great time every year."

The boy had a death grip on Jake's hand and was still pumping away.

"Is Clint Scully going to be at the Gold Buckle?" Kevin asked.

"Sure. I'm expecting Clint anytime now. Joe Watley arrived a couple of days ago. Cody's here. Wayne and Trace are here. Ramon is arriving later in the week. More are coming in every day."

The boy was ready to rocket out of the chair at that news. "Oh, wow! Oh, cool! This is awesome!"

"Kevin, Mr. Dixon is going to be needing his hand back," his mother said, her green eyes twinkling.

Jake laughed and stood up slowly, his knees and back grinding painfully. Every bone in his thirty-two-year-old frame ached like a sore tooth. He had one month to heal from his latest round of injuries and start his comeback. The next three months of the tour would be crucial. Just one more World Finals in Vegas…

"It's fine with me if he calls me Jake, and you, too, ma'am. We're not formal here."

Kevin finally released his hand. "What's wrong, Jake? You in pain? It was Scooter who stomped on your legs, right?"

"Scooter got me pretty good in Oklahoma City, but I think the worst came from Prickly Pear way back at the Billings event. White Whale made it worse in Loughlin. But I'll be okay."

"Just another day at the office. Right?"

He choked back a laugh. "Right, Kevin."

Jake felt uncomfortable talking about himself. Besides he had no business talking about his minor injuries when the boy was in a wheelchair.

He hadn't read all the files yet, so he didn't know Kevin's history. His folks were sticklers about keeping a file on each kid enrolled in the Wheelchair Rodeo program. Everyone who worked with the kids was expected to read each one. Then they'd be turned over to his pal, Dr. Mike Trotter, the resident physician for the week, for his review.

"Shall we head over to pick up your gear?" Jake stepped around to push Kevin's chair, and Beth was more than willing to give it up.

She smiled up at him. "Thank you."

"You look tired," Jake said, heading for the baggage claim area.

"It was a long flight."

"Arizona's pretty far away. Pretty country, though. Their rodeo is the best, but I've been there a couple other times too."

"Really, Jake?"

Beth gave Kevin a nudge on the shoulder. "See? Arizona's not so boring. Jake Dixon likes it."

"Yeah," Kevin said.

Pieces of luggage were starting their trip on the rubber conveyer belt, and people rushed to claim a spot along its path. There was no room for a wheelchair and two more people.

"We're in no rush. Right?" Jake asked.

"Not at all. We're on vacation," Beth said with a long sigh.

It was a long way to travel, but her weariness seemed more bone deep than it should have been just from the flight. She could use some color in her cheeks and some sweet Wyoming air, and maybe some good old-fashioned rocking on the front porch of her cabin.

"Well, if it ain't Jake Dixon."

Jake spun around in the direction of the deep, booming voice. Harvey Trumble, editor of the *Wyoming Journal,* stood with two suitcases in hand and the usual grimace on his face.

Everyone within earshot turned to stare, including Beth and Kevin.

Just his luck. "Go catch your plane, Harvey. Now's not a good time."

Harvey dropped his suitcases and clenched his fists.

Shoot. Jake didn't want to fight the man. Not with the kid so close, watching his every move and looking at him as if he were some kind of hero. Besides, Harvey had a good fifty pounds on him, and even though Jake was younger, he couldn't risk a new injury.

"I have things to do, Harvey. I'm not looking for a fight."

"You gotta be drunk to fight me, Jake? Like you were when you almost killed my boy?"

Jake glanced over at the two arrivals. Kevin's eyes were as wide as saucers. Beth stared at him as if rattlers were sprouting from his ears. She stepped in front of Jake, took the handles of Kevin's chair and wheeled him to the far end of the luggage belt.

Jake grabbed Harvey's arm and yanked him out the front door of the airport, away from most of the crowd.

"Like I told you before, Harvey, Keith had his hands all over a young lady, who told him to stop no less than three times."

Jake had to calm down before he punched him. If he hit him, Harvey would see to it that it was front-page news. Just like the article he wrote about how Jake's sponsors were dropping him faster than an eight-second ride.

Jake dodged his wild punch. "C'mon, Harvey. Not now."

"You didn't have to break my boy's arm."

"I didn't. I admit that I punched Keith after he took a swing at me. But then it turned into a big free-for-all. Someone hit him on the head with a beer bottle. When he fell, he broke his arm. Keith is okay. He's getting a lot of sympathy and still managing to paw the ladies at the Last Chance, even with one arm in a cast."

Harvey pushed Jake out of his way.

"You're nothing but a has-been!" Harvey yelled. "You're a drunk, Jake Dixon, and you hurt my boy." Not taking his eyes off Jake, he backed up to the automatic doors of the airport and went inside.

It was then that Jake noticed Beth and Kevin outside. They both stared at him. Beth's face was ghostly white, her lips pinched. Kevin was motionless in his chair, so unlike the animated, excited boy who'd got off the plane.

"Sorry you had to hear that," Jake said, feeling lower than the stuff he scraped off his boots. He didn't know exactly what they'd heard, except for Harvey's parting slam.

"Maybe we should take a taxi to the ranch." Beth's words faded into the air, then she stood tall and raised her chin. "I'm sorry if this offends you, Mr. Dixon, but I have to ask. Have you been drinking? Kevin and I will not be riding with anyone who has been drinking."

"I haven't been drinking," Jake said softly, meeting her eyes.

"Mom, he's Jake Dixon. Jake Dixon! He doesn't do stuff like that."

The adoration was back in the kid's eyes, but Jake sure as hell didn't feel like a hero.

"My truck's right there." He nodded in the direction of his black half-ton pickup. "It's a good hour-and-a-half ride to the Gold Buckle over some pretty rough roads. The taxis won't make the trip out there." He still saw the disbelief in her eyes. "Ma'am, I haven't been drinking."

She touched Kevin's hair protectively. "I made a mistake once before." After a long, hard, evaluating look into Jake's eyes, she said, "All right, Mr. Dixon. All right. I'm going to believe you—unless I find out otherwise."

"Please call me Jake."

"I'd rather not."

Chapter Two

What am I doing? Beth thought as she looked out the truck window at the tall green grass. Cattle dotted the pastures, and mountains loomed in the distance just like they did around Lizard Rock, Arizona.

With one elbow stuck out the window and the other hand draped casually over the wheel, Jake drove down what seemed like an endless highway, patiently answering Kevin's infinite number of questions.

She stole a glance at him out of the corner of her eye. He had a strong jaw and a trace of beard that made him look a little like an outlaw. Long, strong legs were packed into tight, worn jeans, and he wore a crisp, white long-sleeved shirt with the top three buttons undone. He wore a gold buckle, almost as big as a saucer, on his belt.

He looked just like the posters and pictures that were

hanging from every free space in Kevin's tiny room. Because she'd read every article about him for the past several years, she felt like she knew him, inside and out.

She had always thought he was handsome, but she hadn't been prepared for how masculine and virile he was in person. She had never realized that his blue eyes glittered like the turquoise sky above, or that his low, rich voice would make every bone in her body vibrate.

From the top of his hat to the slightly curled tip of his dusty boots, Jake Dixon looked every bit the cowboy that he was.

She remembered how he had picked Kevin up from his wheelchair and gently placed him in the front seat of his pickup—and Kevin was no lightweight by any means. She had heard him catch his breath after he straightened his back, and she had seen him grimace. He also had a noticeable limp. Bull riding was taking a heavy toll on him.

No doubt his drinking didn't help matters, either. That was something that wasn't mentioned in the magazines.

Her hands tightened into fists. She had heard all that she'd wanted to hear outside the airport. *"You're a drunk, and you hurt my son."*

Those same words had been running through her mind when she stood at Brad's grave and while Kevin endured one operation after another.

She wrapped an arm around her son's shoulder and pulled him closer to her. She hadn't protected him from his own father, but she would protect him from Jake Dixon.

Her heart sank as she thought about the Wheelchair

Rodeo program and how it was to start in two days. The literature she had received indicated that Jake had started the program, and he saw to everything personally.

How was she going to trust him with Kevin?

"Okay, Mom?" Kevin asked, breaking through her reverie.

"Hmm? What?" she asked.

"Jake said that he'd show me around the ranch when we get there. And that I can pick out my own horse from the remuda. Hear that, Mom? *The remuda.* And I get to take care of my horse all week!"

"That's great," she mumbled without enthusiasm. How was she going to tell her son that she didn't want him near his hero?

"Okay, Mom?"

She needed time to think. She wanted to know more about the real Jake Dixon. She wanted to observe him. She didn't want to hand her son over to him and trust him, the way she had trusted Brad. Not with what she had just heard about him.

Jake must have seen her hesitation.

"I'll take good care of Kevin. And you're welcome to come along. Right, Kev?"

Her stomach clenched. No one ever called him Kev, except Brad.

"Yeah, c'mon, Mom. Come with us."

She could never say no to Kevin when he looked at her with those big brown eyes. And she didn't want to throw a wet blanket on his excitement. Maybe it was unfair of her to compare Jake to Brad.

"Sure. I'd love to," she reluctantly agreed.

"Yippee!" Kevin shouted.

The two of them went back to talking about who rode what bull for a ninety-point ride, and who was on the injured list. From the look on Jake's rugged face, Kevin's knowledge about the sport surprised him. If only Kevin were that good in English and math.

She laid her head back on the seat of the big truck and listened to their conversation. Kevin was bubbly and happy, and Jake was adding to his excitement, so much so that it was almost contagious.

"There it is! The Gold Buckle Ranch!" Kevin shouted. "It's a real ranch!"

A slender, pretty woman in jeans and a navy-blue sweatshirt stood waving on the front porch of a log ranch house. Beside her was a tall, handsome man in jeans and a flannel shirt. They both had warm, welcoming smiles.

"My folks," Jake said. "Em and Dex Dixon."

She and Kevin waved back.

Dex opened the truck door and helped her out. "Welcome to the Gold Buckle, Beth." He bent his head to peer inside the truck. "And this young cowboy must be Kevin."

"Yessir!" Kevin said.

Kevin scooted to the end of the seat, and Beth let out a gasp when it looked as if he might just jump down from the truck.

"Whoa, young man!" Dex said. "Hang on there."

Jake already had Kevin's chair and the two men were helping Kevin out when Emily gathered Beth in a hearty hug.

"It's so nice to meet you. I feel like I know you already from Kevin's letter," Emily said.

Beth let herself relax and enjoy the warm greeting.

There wasn't a day that went by that she didn't wish she had a mother who would hug her like that and who she could talk to and confide in, especially now, when she was so worried about Kevin. But Carla Tisdale Phillips O'Brien Fontelli had never been that kind of mother, and she never hugged.

"Welcome, Kevin!" Emily said as the boy beamed up at her. She bent down and gave him a hug too. "I have you in the Trail Boss Cabin. That's the far one in those big pine trees. It has a lot of privacy. Now come into my kitchen for a bite to eat, and Jake will drop your bags inside the cabin. That okay with you, Jake?"

"Sure."

"Then come back for a bite to eat when you're done," she added.

"I have to talk to Joe and check on the mustang. Then I'll be in," Jake replied. "After that, I promised Kevin that he could pick out his horse for the week. Then I'm going to show him and his mom around the ranch."

He looked at Beth and tweaked his hat brim. She watched as he walked away. His limp was more prominent now. His shirt didn't have a wrinkle on it as it stretched across broad shoulders and a muscled back.

Most of all, Jake Dixon was born to wear jeans.

"It's a beautiful place," Beth told Jake as she looked out at the grounds of the Gold Buckle Ranch from the porch of the Trail Boss Cabin. "So big. I've never seen anything like it."

The mountains seemed closer now and rocky. Those in the far distance had a cap of snow. The ranch was nestled in a valley with pine trees to the right and a field of grass that reached to the mountains to the left. Among the pines, a dozen little log cabins were strung along a glittering creek like charms on a bracelet.

The Trail Boss Cabin, deep in the pines, was postcard perfect. It was made out of rough logs, pine probably. Lacy curtains graced the windows, in stark contrast to the rugged logs. Two rocking chairs and a hammock were on the porch, just begging to be occupied.

Hundreds of cows and a dozen horses lowered their heads to graze on a slight hill about a half mile away. Closer were several other buildings of different shapes and sizes. The biggest was the barn with a corral to the side of it. Horses grouped together under the shade of several large trees. Some looked over the fence as if they, too, were awaiting guests.

She took a deep breath. The air was pure and held the scent of pine.

The Trail Boss Cabin was just as cute inside as she had thought it would be. It had two bedrooms and a screened-in back porch overlooking the creek. Pink geranium ivy cascaded from terra-cotta pots on the steps leading down from the porch. She could hear the rushing stream behind and on the right side of the cabin. Like all of the other cabins, it had a wheelchair ramp.

Inside, a stone fireplace took over one wall of the living room, which flowed into the kitchen. The appliances were old but brilliantly clean. The inside walls were varnished, knotty pine planks, aged to a golden hue. The bedrooms and the bathroom were down a small hall.

"Hey, Mom, it's bigger than our apartment," Kevin yelled from one of the bedrooms.

"It seems like it is."

"Wouldn't you like to stay here forever?" Kevin came toward her, the wheels of his chair rolling effortlessly down the hardwood floor.

Beth sighed. It was a homey place in which to live. So calm, so quiet. It seemed like she could reach out and touch the mountains. However, she had to make a living and that living was in Lizard Rock, Arizona.

Heaven knows, she had enough bills to pay. She lived free at the apartments and received a small salary for being the rental agent and manager, but she had to be there to do her job. She was lucky that Inez, her boss, had given her this time off. Unfortunately, it was without pay, and that was going to set her budget plans back to the Stone Age.

"That's not possible, Kevin," she said. "I have a job back in Arizona and you have school. Remember, this is just a vacation."

"But if we lived here, it would be like a vacation all the time," Kevin said. "Huh, Jake?"

Jake deposited their suitcases near the kitchen table. "Running a ranch is a lot of work, Kev. Not every day is a vacation."

Beth could have hugged him for that answer.

"But there's not a better job in the world," Jake added. "Other than riding bulls. And there's no state prettier than Wyoming."

If only he had stopped while he was ahead.

They walked back onto the porch, and Beth sat down in one of the rocking chairs. Jake stood by Kevin's side near the railing.

Kevin pointed to a long building. "That's the bunkhouse. Right, Jake? I wish I could stay there with the cowboys tonight—"

"The Trail Boss Cabin is perfectly fine," Beth interrupted before Jake could even answer. She might as well nip that idea in the bud.

When Wheelchair Rodeo started in a couple of days, he'd be moving into the bunkhouse with the other boys in the program, and that was soon enough. Besides, Beth still had mixed feelings about Kevin leaving her watchful eye.

"How many cowboys work here, Mr. Dixon?" she asked, trying to be polite but secretly hoping that he'd disappear. Surely, there were other guests who needed his attention.

"That depends. The door is always open to cowboys who are healing from their injuries, or those who need a place to stay for whatever reason. Mostly, they stop by for a few days for some of my mother's pies or Cookie's cooking. In exchange for room and board, they help out around the place."

"Even more come for the Gold Buckle Challenge. Right, Jake?"

"That's right, Kev. But they come for both rodeos. They like helping out with Wheelchair Rodeo maybe even more than they like riding in the Gold Buckle Challenge. Some of them bring their families and camp out in the upper pasture. Some just crash at the bunkhouse. It's like a reunion."

"They wouldn't come if it wasn't for you, Jake," Kevin said.

"Maybe. That's nice of you to say, Kev. So, how about a real tour?"

"Cool! C'mon, Mom!"

Kevin flew down the ramp before she even got out of the rocker. She was just going to remind him to be careful when Jake held out his hands to help her up.

Without thinking, she put her hands into his. They were rough, callused. Hands that did physical work, ranch work, real work. Brad's hands had always been soft and perfectly manicured—but then, Brad wasn't a cowboy. He'd been a stockbroker.

Although she was on her feet, she held on to him for a moment longer than necessary to take her measure of the man she would have to trust. The man who would be taking care of her son.

Jake met her gaze with steady, unflinching eyes. Eyes that weren't bloodshot like Brad's had always been.

"Is that the barn? Oh, wow! It's the barn, Mom!" Kevin called.

Realizing that she was holding on to Jake way too long, she dropped his hands. "Wait for us, Kevin!" she shouted back.

Jake smiled. "I've never seen anyone so thrilled about a barn," he said, as they walked down a cleared path.

They stopped at the gate of the corral. Several horses walked over, most of them sniffing Kevin and Jake. Even to Beth's untrained eye, the long-legged, satin-coated horses looked like beauties.

"They know that I usually have a treat for them." Jake dipped a hand in the pocket of his shirt and handed Kevin a piece of a carrot. "Hold it flat on your hand and don't be scared when their big yellow teeth come at you."

"I'm not scared," he said, but he had a white-knuckled grip on the arm of his wheelchair. His other hand was flat, his face a study in concentration.

"They won't hurt you," Jake said. "Just reach out. Keep your hand flat."

Kevin did it, and when the horse gently took the carrot, Kevin let out a little squeal. "Cool!"

Jake turned to Beth. "How about you?"

Beth nodded, eager to try. She held out her hand and he placed a piece of carrot on it. The horses pushed closer, each nosing for the food. She picked out a horse who was more patient than the others and opened her hand.

Jake moved behind her and put his hand under hers. "Keep your hand flat."

It was a harmless gesture, but she could feel the warmth of his chest on her back, could smell the scent of his spicy aftershave, the warm wisps of his breath on the side of her face.

When the carrots were gone, Kevin turned to Jake. "Which horse is going to be mine?"

"None of these. They're not ready yet. But there's a couple in the barn you might like."

He tugged back two enormous wooden doors. The smell of horses and hay drifted around them.

Kevin gave a breathy "Oh, wow!" and wheeled into the barn.

Beth inhaled. "This reminds me of when I was a kid and I lived in central New York—my parents used to take me to the state fair."

Jake looked at her with interest, waiting for her to continue.

"I waited all summer for the fair. I couldn't wait to go through the horse barns and look at all the beautiful horses. I'd pick one out and pretend it was mine. Then I'd watch the horse shows and cheer my horse to victory."

"Now I know where Kevin gets his love of horses."

Jake smiled, and she could see tiny lines at the corners of his eyes that were white against the dark tan of his face.

She smiled back. "I've always liked horses." She paused, thinking back. "When Kevin was little, several times during the day he'd hand me a book, crawl up on my lap and ask me to read to him. I read every book with a horse or a pony on the cover a hundred times over. I'd take him to horse shows and rodeos when they were nearby. He just loved going."

The memories that the barn smells triggered washed over her, all warm and comforting. Those were some of the best times of her life, just Kevin and her, and that's the way she liked it.

Kevin craned his neck as he wheeled down the cement walkway of the barn. He didn't know where to look first. On both sides were stalls, and most of the horses hung their heads over the half-door. On each door was a wooden sign with the horse's name in black print.

"That one there is a beauty," he said. "Wow! So is that one! And that one!"

Jake was patient with Kevin. As they came to each stall, Kevin had to pet the horse and call it by name.

After a while, Beth caught Jake's eye. "Can I speak with you, Mr. Dixon?"

Nodding, he left Kevin petting a horse and walked over toward her.

"About the horse—"

Jake held a hand up. "I promise you, Kevin's horse will be gentle. All the horses in this barn are hand-picked for Wheelchair Rodeo. I work with them myself. Don't worry."

"Easy for you to say," she said. "He's not your son."

"No, but I'll take care of him as if he were."

She met his gaze. His blue eyes were as cool and as refreshing as a spring day, and he truly seemed to care about Kevin.

So then why couldn't she let herself trust him completely?

Because she had trusted her son to a man with a drinking problem before, and Kevin was almost killed. And the man had died.

Jake glanced down the long row of horses and shouted, "You might like Cheyenne, Kev, or the black horse in stall three. Check them out." Then he turned back to Beth and lowered his voice. "Look, I don't know all of what you heard at the airport, but don't pay any attention to it."

"I heard that you were drunk and hurt a man."

"I wasn't drunk. I had a few beers, yes. I had some words with someone, and then suddenly we were in the middle of a free-for-all." Jake sighed and looked away. After several seconds, his gaze returned to her. "Look, Wheelchair Rodeo begins the day after tomorrow, so if you're having second thoughts about trusting me with Kevin, you'd better tell me now."

She met his direct gaze. "I'm having second thoughts."

"Fair enough." He nodded. "Then take him out of the program."

"It would break his heart," she said. "You're his hero. He idolizes you."

"Lady, I'm no one's hero. It's all I can do these days to get up every morning." He was speaking through gritted teeth. "And I might be a lot of things, but I'm not a drunk."

That was just what Brad had always said.

Beth swallowed hard and glanced at Kevin to make sure he was out of hearing range. She knew she had angered Jake Dixon, but she had good reasons for not trusting him—or anyone, for that matter—with her son.

Maybe she owed him an explanation. "His father was an alcoholic," she said. "He picked Kevin up at a friend's birthday party. Brad was drunk and he drove his car into the cement of a bridge. Brad died and Kevin lived. After four operations in two years, Kevin's still in a wheelchair. The doctors don't understand why."

"Oh...shoot..." He took off his hat and raked his fingers through his hair, then plopped the hat back on his head. "I'm sorry," he said, watching Kevin. "But now at least I understand why you hate drinking." He paused. "He'll never get out of the chair?"

He touched her arm when she didn't answer right away. It was an unexpected, comforting gesture. The look on his face was concerned and sympathetic. She wondered yet again if she was judging him too harshly.

She took a deep breath and jumped in. "Kevin's last operation was supposed to work, but obviously it didn't." When the tears started to sting her eyes, she blinked them back. "He's idolized you since he first met you at the Tucson rodeo. He was five years old. You paid attention to him, listened to him, and you gave him a red bandana. He's never forgotten that, and one of the things that kept him going was his dream of coming to the Wheelchair Rodeo."

"I'm honored, but—"

Beth held up an index finger. "Oh, there's much more. Ever since then, he's watched bull riding constantly on TV, looking for you, cheering you on. When he was in the hospital, he fought to stay awake to watch you being interviewed on Letterman during one of his hospital stays. Your fan club sent him a special autographed picture that has never left his sight. He wears your clothes. His room is covered in pictures of Jake Dixon. He thinks you're the greatest thing since school recess."

Jake met her gaze. "I don't know what to say."

"You can promise me that you'll be the hero he thinks you are."

Jake stared down at the floor. "I can't promise that."

He shifted from foot to foot, and Beth sensed that he wanted to get as far away from her as possible.

"I'm just a cowboy. That's all. I can guarantee you that he'll have a good time at the ranch. I can teach him how to ride and rope and cook over a campfire, but if he needs a hero, he'd best look up to Jimmy Watley or Clint Scully or another cowboy."

"But it's you he idolizes."

He shook his head as if he were shaking her words out, and walked toward Kevin, his boots making dull clicking noises on the cement.

She trailed behind him. Nobody's hero? Kevin was only one little boy among thousands who worshiped the ground he walked on. He was the primary reason why

Kevin worked so hard to get better. "Jake Dixon is tough, Mom. I am, too," Kevin had told her.

She owed Jake Dixon. She owed him a lot.

"Have you picked one out yet?" Jake said to Kevin. "Remember, you have to take care of the horse all week. That means brushing, feeding, watering and taking care of the tack. Got it?"

"I can do it, Jake. I promise!"

"Then who will it be, Kev?" Jake asked.

"Killer."

Beth closed the distance between them. *"Killer?"*

"Actually, his full name is Killer Bee, but we call him Killer for short," Jake explained.

That didn't make her feel any better. She didn't want Kevin riding on a horse named Killer, even if it was a cute black horse with soulful black eyes.

She would have called him Thunder, like another fictional horse of her childhood she'd discovered in a library book. Her Thunder was a shiny, black horse with four white socks. She read the book over and over again until she just about had it memorized.

She looked over the stall door to see if Killer Bee had white socks. He didn't, but he was still a beautiful horse.

Kevin fidgeted in his chair. "Will you take him out of the stall, Jake? I want to look at him all over."

"Okay, Kev."

With Kevin on the edge of his seat, Jake led Killer Bee out of his stall.

The horse sniffed at Kevin's shirt as the boy giggled and reached out to pet him. "Just think," said Kevin, "he's mine for a week."

Jake raised an eyebrow, met Beth's eyes and waited for her reply.

She took a deep breath and prayed that she wouldn't regret her decision. Kevin's doctor felt that the horseback riding would be good for him, would strengthen his muscles. That would be wonderful for his broken body, but she knew that the Gold Buckle Ranch experience would do even more for Kevin's morale.

"Yes, Kevin. He's yours while we are here. Make sure you listen to Mr. Dixon—Jake—and learn how to take care of him."

Jake gave a slight nod, obviously pleased with her decision. "Well, buckaroo, I'd best get you and your mom back to the Trail Boss Cabin so you both can get some rest."

He put Killer back into his stall. "If I have time tomorrow, we can get a riding lesson in and maybe even a roping lesson. You can get a jump on the rest of the kids."

"Cool. I brought my *official* Jake Dixon rope with me."

Jake shrugged. "Huh?"

"I bought it from your *official* Web site for Kevin's ninth birthday," Beth explained.

"Oh. I forgot about that. My fan club runs the Web site," he mumbled, then said to Kevin, "I'm sure it's a good rope if you bought it from my *official* Web site." He grinned.

"Well, it's time we went to bed, cowboy," Beth said. "It's been a long day."

Jake did a double-take, raised an eyebrow and

pushed back his hat with a thumb. His eyes twinkled in amusement.

"Kevin," she clarified, grinning in spite of herself. It was hard not to like Jake. "It's time for bed, *Kevin.*"

Chapter Three

Beth woke to the scent of pine. A breeze lightly tossed the lace curtains. Sunlight flickered on her face, and she smiled. What a nice way to wake up. But why wake up yet? She turned over, scrunched the pillow to the perfect shape under her head and closed her eyes again.

"That's awesome, Jake."

Jake. That name again. She had dreamed of the tall, lean cowboy with the lazy grin and the sexy blue eyes all night. Now she woke up to his name drifting on the breeze.

She even remembered saying the same phrase—*"That's awesome, Jake"*—in her dream when he... when they...

"Totally cool, Jake."

She had never said *that* in her dream.

"Kevin?" She shot up in bed. "Kevin?"

"Out here, Mom!"

"Where?" She tore out of the bedroom, her heart pounding wildly in her chest. She ran into his bedroom, but he wasn't there. She checked the bathroom. "Kevin?" Barely breathing, she raced to the door and tore it open.

"Hi, Mom!"

Her son was astride a big black horse—Killer Bee. He was belted into some kind of special saddle with a high back and sides. Jake Dixon was standing next to him with reins in his hand. They both were petting the horse and smiling like they hadn't a care in the world.

When she caught something extra in Jake's grin, she realized that she was barefoot on the front porch of the Trail Boss Cabin in her red satin nightgown with spaghetti straps, a buy-one-get-one-free special from Wal-Mart.

She crossed her arms in front of her, sure that Jake could see how cold she actually was.

"Kevin," she began in her scolding-mom tone.

"Aw…don't be mad at me. I got up early and saw Jake at the corral. We had breakfast in the bunkhouse with all the cowboys. It was so cool, Mom. Joe Watley was there. And Gilbert. And Ty Watson, T.J., and Trace and…"

She held her hand up to stop him from naming every cowboy in the bunkhouse. "You should have asked me, Kevin. Also, I don't think you should be taking up so much of Mr. Dixon's time."

She studied Jake. He was clean-shaven. She looked for signs of a hangover, but his eyes were bright and clear. He tipped his hat back with a thumb, a gesture she had seen more than once. It was as if he were saying *"Look me over. I don't care."*

So she looked.

"Kev's not bothering me. I enjoy his company."

"That may be true, but Kevin shouldn't have left the cabin without letting me know."

"He said he didn't want to wake you, and that you were snoring up a storm." Jake chuckled.

"I certainly do not snore!" Beth protested.

"Mom, you were sucking the walls in."

She couldn't help but laugh. Running a hand through her hair, she realized that it was tangled. In spite of the cold, she felt a warm flush as Jake Dixon's blatant gaze swept over her again.

"Mr. Dixon, may I impose on you to watch Kevin a while longer while I get dressed?"

"Of course. I'm just going to let Kevin walk Killer around the paddock. Take your time."

"Be careful, Kevin. Nothing fancy, okay? And listen to Mr. Dixon."

"I will. I will." His voice had that "quit nagging me" tone to it, but she couldn't help herself. She always worried.

As she was about to go back into the cabin, Emily Dixon turned the corner and waved to her. "Beth, you're just the person I'm looking for."

"Good morning, Emily." She slumped over in another attempt to make her nightgown appear longer. "Please come inside. I need to get dressed."

"Good morning, boys." She gave Kevin and Jake a wave. Turning back to Beth, she said, "Stay put. I'll make it quick. I need another volunteer for the overnight campout, a woman to assist the girls in the program. Now, I know you are on vacation, and you need a break from— Well, I wouldn't ask if I wasn't desperate. Can you help us out?"

"Certainly," she said without hesitation. If she was assisting Wheelchair Rodeo, she could keep an eye on Kevin.

"But, Mrs. Dixon, my mom doesn't know how to ride," Kevin said. "She won't be able to go on the trail ride and campout."

"I can take care of teaching your mother how to ride," Jake said.

His blue eyes sparkled in the morning sun like twin sapphires. She didn't particularly want to be in Jake Dixon's company all that much. In just the short time she'd known him, she was already feeling a pull toward him. And now she was having erotic dreams about him. Why?

He was stirring up feelings that she hadn't known she had, as well as fears about Brad and his drinking that she'd tried to bury, along with her husband.

She saw an amused look on Emily Dixon's face. It was as if she knew that Beth was trying to fight an attraction to Jake.

"Thank you, son." Emily kissed Jake on the cheek as she walked by him, then she was off down the path that led to the ranch house. "Breakfast is still being served in the mess hall, Beth," she said over her shoulder as she disappeared around the corner.

Beth was suddenly too nervous to eat. "I'll be ready in a half hour," she said to Jake. "I guess I should pick out a horse."

"I'll pick one out for you if you'd like," Jake said.

She nodded and turned to go into the cabin, then turned back. "Jake? Mr. Dixon?"

"Yes, ma'am?" He waited patiently for her to continue.

She didn't know if she could ask the question she wanted to without sounding like a fool. But what the heck? "Do you have a black horse with four white socks?"

He studied her as if trying to figure out the reason for her request. To his credit, he didn't laugh. "I believe I do."

Well, she was in this far, she might as well let him think she was completely out of her mind. "Do you have a horse with four white socks named Thunder, by any chance?" she asked.

"Thunder?" He raised an eyebrow.

His eyes met hers. The moment hung between them and then he smiled. A look of gentle understanding crossed his tanned face.

"Yeah. Yes. I do have a horse named Thunder. And he has four white socks."

She knew he wasn't telling the truth, but the white lie moved him up a couple of notches in her estimation.

"Could I have that horse?" she asked.

"Sure."

Smiling, she hurried into the cabin and shut the door. Leaning against it, she clamped a hand over her mouth to control the giddiness that bubbled up from somewhere. She felt happy, euphoric, as if she were flying. She released her hand and her laughter overflowed.

Maybe her strange mood was due to her relief that Kevin was okay. Maybe it was because she was going to ride a horse after all these years. Maybe it was because she got a good night's sleep. But it was not, definitely not, because she had dreamed about Jake all night, then awoken to see him so attentive toward her son.

Kevin would have memories that he'd cherish forever, and she'd always be grateful to Jake Dixon for that.

She was glad that she was going to help out with Wheelchair Rodeo. Since they'd both received a "scholarship" to WR, it gave her the opportunity to contribute something to the program. WR was something special.

She rushed to her room, plucked a pair of jeans and a T-shirt out of her suitcase and hurried to the shower.

Twenty minutes later, refreshed and dressed, she stepped out onto the porch of her cabin. She walked toward the barn and saw Jake sitting on the corral fence, waiting for her.

Jake felt Beth's gaze on the back of his neck, watching his every move with Kevin. A prickle of irritation shot through him. What did she think he was going to do? Toss the boy, wheelchair and all, into his pickup and hit the honky-tonks?

Finally, with her reluctant permission, he handed Kevin and Killer over to bronc rider K.C. Morris and sent them to the Chisholm Trail, a short, easy walking path that meandered behind the dining hall and the bunkhouse, then circled back to the barn.

That would be enough for Kevin for the day. He was using new muscles, and Jake didn't want to overwhelm the little guy. Then K.C. could help Kev unsaddle Killer, brush him down and clean the tack.

"There isn't anything K.C. doesn't know about kids or horses," he reassured Beth. "He comes from a family of nine kids and owns some of the finest horses in Texas."

That didn't seem to impress her. It was Kevin's hopeful "Please, Mom?" that did it.

Jake felt sorry for the kid. Although he liked the thought that Beth would be helping out on the overnight, she was a bit too overprotective and stifling. He'd bet his last saddle that Kevin needed a break from her.

And she needed to relax.

As Kevin disappeared behind the pines, she bit her nails.

"You're next," Jake said, jumping down from the fence. He winced from the pain.

"Maybe when Kevin comes back."

"Beth, Kevin's fine. He's on a short, easy walking trail that we call the Chisolm Trail. I guarantee he's having the time of his life. C'mon, it's your turn. You're going to love the horse I picked out for you."

He gave a shrill whistle and a horse came trotting over. He watched Beth's face for her reaction. It was just as he'd expected. She broke into a big grin, and he swore she was going to jump right out of her skin.

Sidewinder, with his two white socks, belonged to his friend Dan Montague's son, Danny. Luckily, they'd loaned the gentle horse to Wheelchair Rodeo, along with several others they'd raised on their neighboring spread. Jake had painted two more socks on Sidewinder with white shoe polish. Beth's bright eyes and grin told him that it was well worth the trouble.

"She's a beauty, Jake. I don't know how to thank you."

"She's a 'he.'" He shook his head. "I can see my work is cut out for me!"

"What's his real name?"

"Thunder."

"No. Really—"

"Thunder," Jake insisted. "And he's ready for some exercise. Let's go saddle him up."

Jake opened the corral door for Beth. As Thunder nudged Beth's shirt pocket with his nose, she stepped back laughing.

He took her hand and dropped some sugar cubes onto her palm. "Flat on your hand."

"I remember."

His hand skimmed hers, and he felt as if he'd gone eight seconds with Prickly Pear again. When she looked up at him with her glittering green eyes, he felt as if he were free-falling. Sooner or later he knew he'd hit the ground and eat dirt.

Why couldn't he just walk away from Beth Conroy? He understood why he was drawn to her son. He saw the man he used to be in Kevin's adoring eyes—not an over-the-hill, washed-up bull rider who'd been keeping the Justin Sports Medicine Program busy. Hell, Beth was everything he didn't need—overprotective, stifling and bossy.

He didn't know the answer, but he was going to push it out of his mind and concentrate on Wheelchair Rodeo for now. If it killed him, he was going to be on top again.

He'd win his event this Saturday, the Jake Dixon Gold Buckle Challenge. Then he'd pick up the PBR tour in August. He'd win the bull-riding Finals in Vegas in October. Maybe after that, he'd retire. Then again, maybe not.

But if he did, he would retire a winner.

"I'll show you how to saddle and bridle your horse," Jake said.

Beth signaled her muscles to relax and not bunch. A nervous giggle escaped. She tried to cover it with a cough.

"I'd bet my boots that you've never saddled a horse before," Jake said.

"Hope your socks are clean, because I'm going to win your boots." She reached up and petted Thunder. "I did saddle a horse—once—many years ago. And I certainly read enough books about it when I was a kid. It's probably like riding a bike. "

"Don't worry. I'm not going to let you do it alone, not the first time—but you'll learn. Just like Kevin will learn. So will the rest of the kids who are cleared to ride. They'll get a lot of help, and they'll do what they can."

His hands moved to her waist. She jumped. He was only getting her into position, but her heart pumped hard, sending heat through her veins. His touch was harmless, not intimate at all. Yet it had been a long time since a man other than Brad had touched her. Every nerve in her body was humming.

Jake lifted an orange-and-gray blanket that was draped over a metal stand and handed it to her. "Put that on his back. It's made of heavy wool—cushions the horse from saddle sores and absorbs the sweat."

She took the blanket and placed it on Thunder.

"Now the saddle. It weighs about thirty-five pounds. Can you handle it?"

"Kevin weighs much more than that, and I lift him."

He felt the muscles in her upper arm and grinned. "I'm impressed. You're a tough lady."

"I just do what I have to."

The smile left his face. "It must be difficult for you."

"He's my son."

"If you don't mind me saying so, you overprotect him."

She stared at him until she finally found her voice. "What gives you the right to judge me, Mr. Dixon?"

"I can tell that—"

"Do you have a degree in child psychology?" She picked up the saddle and flung it on Thunder's back. She could have flung Jake Dixon up there, too.

"I see you—"

"Mr. Dixon, what I think you need to do is concentrate on roping and riding the range and doing whatever else a cowboy does. Leave the child rearing to someone who has a child to rear."

"How do you know I don't have a child? Or a good dozen of them?"

"All your publicity says..." A vein pumped on his temple. She'd hit a nerve.

"Don't believe everything you read," he snapped. He took a couple of deep breaths and pushed his hat back. "Look, Beth, I didn't mean to upset you. I was only going to say that you need to give the kid and yourself a break."

Maybe she *was* too overprotective of Kevin, but that

was because she was determined not to let anything more happen to her son. She realized that she couldn't guarantee she'd be able to keep him safe forever, but she could sure as hell try.

"Let's get back to the lesson," she said.

He held his hands up in surrender. "I'll drop it." He grinned. "For now."

"Forever."

He moved his hat back to its usual position. "Lift the left stirrup and hook it over the horn. Good. Grab the cinch strap. Good. Pull it through. Good. You got it. Nothing to it. Now tighten it up. Harder."

She grunted and tightened the strap as much as she could. She wasn't a weakling. After the accident she had developed muscles that she hadn't known she had.

"Now what?"

Jake gripped the saddle horn and jerked it. "Not good enough. Thunder puffed himself up."

"He did what?"

"He doesn't like being cinched, so he swells himself up. Brace yourself with a knee against his ribs—" he pointed "—about here."

"I can't do that!"

"It won't hurt him."

"I still can't do it."

"Okay." He nudged Thunder with a knee. "Don't make me get ugly in front of the lady, horse. She adores you. Knock it off."

Jake easily tightened the cinch another few inches.

"Good boy." Jake fed him a piece of carrot and turned to Beth.

He handed her a bridle. "Go for it."

She stared down at the leather and metal in her hand, then at Thunder's big yellow teeth. "I guess you can keep your boots on after all. I don't remember this part."

"Hold the bridle like this, and slip it under his chin and up over his eyes like this."

She tried to concentrate as he demonstrated, but instead she noticed the faint scar that started just below Jake's ear and ran to his jaw.

"This is a split-ear bridle. It goes around each ear. The bit rests forward in the horse's mouth."

He stopped as Thunder's mouth opened. "See? Thunder's used to it. He knows what to do even if you don't."

"Thank goodness."

"You ready to try it?"

"As I'll ever be."

"Relax. He's not going to bite you."

His arms wrapped around her from behind. She could feel every hard muscle, every mountain and valley of his body against hers. His crotch bumped against her backside. She tried not to notice.

Oh, sure.

He helped her guide the bridle into place. "See? Nothing to it," he said.

Why am I so warm?

She turned and found herself staring at Jake's full lips. They turned up into a sly grin.

He was so close, so overwhelmingly masculine, and she had a strong desire to get away from him. She stepped back.

"Drop 'em."

"What?"

"Drop the reins to the ground. Thunder's a cattle

horse. He's trained to stand still when the reins are dropped to the ground."

She just couldn't think around him, and she hated to feel so out of control, so disjointed. "Oh. You want me to drop the reins."

She did as instructed. Thunder stood as still as a statue in a park.

"Ready to ride?"

She nodded, feeling like she was a kid again. She was at the horse barn at the state fair. Only this time, the horse was hers.

He patted the horse's neck. "Cowboy up!"

Her cheeks were flushed. Jake suspected it was because he made her nervous and she wasn't particularly fond of him. But perhaps she was just excited about riding the horse.

She sucked in a deep breath. "I guess this is how Kevin feels. Maybe he's more like me than I've given him credit for."

"Ah, so you're a cowgirl at heart?"

"When I was a girl, I wanted a horse more than anything in the world." She petted Thunder's neck. "We lived in a tract house, so there wasn't enough land for a horse. Even if my father had bought one, he couldn't afford to stable it."

Jake couldn't imagine growing up without horses and cattle. He needed wide-open spaces. "Out here, just about every kid grows up with a horse, or dozens of them."

"This means a lot to me. How can I thank you, Mr. Dixon?"

"By calling me Jake, for heaven's sake."

She started to protest, then her jaws shut. "Okay."

He let out a long, low whistle. "Finally."

He held Sidewinder's…er…Thunder's reins and lightly touched her arm. "Up you go."

Jake gave her a gentle push on her cute behind. She landed in the saddle and grinned down at him. "It's pretty high up here."

"You'll get used to it." He handed her the reins, and she took them. She clutched the saddle horn, her knuckles turning white. "Relax, Beth. Take a deep breath and relax. Thunder won't do anything stupid."

She took a deep breath and looked into his eyes. "But I'm afraid I might."

"I personally tested him for Wheelchair Rodeo. He's a good, calm horse. Just relax and enjoy."

He showed her how to hold the reins. "I'm just going to lead him around the corral until you get used to the motion."

"Ramon!" He cupped his hands and shouted to a group of cowboys who were watching intently. "As long as you're just sitting there looking pretty, would you mind saddling Lance for me?"

One of them jumped down from the fence. "You got it, bro."

Jake continued to walk Thunder around the corral. She noticed that the more they circled, the worse Jake limped. No doubt the loose soil was taking a toll on whatever was wrong with him.

"I'm comfortable now, Jake. I can see you limping. Wait until Ramon brings your horse out."

"Move forward in the saddle."

"Huh?"

"Move forward."

She did, and before she could blink, Jake had swung a leg up behind her and they were both sitting on the saddle. His arms and thighs were tight around her and she felt him snug against her bottom.

She sat up straight and tried to put a breath of air between them, but there was none to be had. She could smell the laundry soap clinging to his shirt and his unique scent, a tantalizing mixture of pine and leather.

He made a clicking sound and moved the reins. Thunder turned and walked, and she felt the animal's hardness against her, rocking…rocking…

"A couple more times and then we'll take a slow ride on the Chisholm Trail," he said.

His voice was low and seductive in her ear. She wanted to lean her head back on his chest and feel the vibration of his deep voice passing through her.

Instead, she struggled to take her mind off him.

She finally found her voice. "I'd like to ride the Chisholm Trail."

"We also have the Santa Fe Trail and the Dixon Trail and a couple more. They go up in level of difficulty. Guests can only go on the trails I approve them for. The cowboys who work here get a copy of my list each morning, and it's posted in the bunkhouse. No one can go to the next trail unless I pass them."

Jake Dixon ran a tight ranch, and against her better judgment she was starting to like him.

But she still wasn't sure she could trust him with her son.

Chapter Four

Ramon led Lance over. Jake steered Thunder to the corral fence and got off using one of the slats. He immediately felt better with the pressure of Beth's body off his groin. If he had spent any more time snug in the saddle with Beth, he would have embarrassed himself.

Beth was watching his every move. He would have thought that she was interested in him, but he knew better. She was taking his measure, and interested in riding Thunder somewhere other than in a circle around the corral.

"Ready for the Chisholm Trail, city slicker?" he asked.

She grinned. "Round 'em up, move 'em out. Lead the way, cowboy."

He liked it when she loosened up and joked with him.

"Our Chisholm Trail goes from behind the mess hall

to behind the cabins. It ends at your cabin. Then we cross the bridge over the Gold Buckle River and end up right back here."

She looked toward where he pointed. "Here comes Kevin!" she said, waving.

"Kevin and K.C. Safe and sound," Jake said. "Kevin has a grin the size of a prize banana. Just like his mother." Her happiness made Jake feel that his time was well spent. "Shall we hit the trail?"

"I'm ready."

"Follow me."

Jake watched Beth's face as she rode. She focused intently, yet she had a look of pure pleasure. A gentle breeze blew her golden hair back from her face, and her lips parted in a slight smile. Her eyes were bright, and she seemed to have more energy than she had the day before.

That's what he liked about the Gold Buckle. It gave the guests the opportunity to experience new things—things they couldn't do at home.

Wheelchair Rodeo was part of that, but to see a sunrise on a cool, crisp Wyoming morning, to see the eagles fly and the mountains up close…well, there was nothing better.

It was a good stress reliever, and Beth Conroy needed to relieve a lot of stress.

Maybe he'd find time to take her on a trail ride of their own. They could camp in the wildflowers at the foot of Old Baldy. Then they'd take a nice, cool skinny-dip in the little creek that runs along the trail. He'd get Cookie to pack one of his special picnic lunches and throw in a cold jug of his homemade lemonade.

He'd build a campfire and they'd sleep under the

stars, snuggled together. He'd catch some fish for breakfast, and he'd filet and cook them while Beth made the coffee….

He had to be loco. Maybe that was his idea of a perfect date, but Beth didn't seem the camping type. She'd probably want to get dressed up and go somewhere fancy. Besides, camping would mean leaving Kevin in the bunkhouse with the cowboys. She'd never agree to that.

And for what he was thinking, he couldn't take Kevin.

But it didn't make sense to get any closer to her. Women liked hearth and home. That was his experience, anyway. Oh, they might like sex once in a while, but basically they really wanted to settle down.

Not him. He followed the rodeos and the bull riding. When he was healthy, he traveled to about forty events a year—about thirty of those were strictly bull-riding events where his ranking qualified him for the Finals in Las Vegas. Another dozen or so were small rodeos where he rode more bulls just to keep in shape.

He was a bull rider. It was more than what he did. It was who he was.

Beth deserved someone who could be a husband to her and a father to Kevin.

Why was he even thinking along those lines? When he was stomped on by White Whale in Loughlin, some of his brains must have leaked out on the arena dirt.

No settling down for him. Even if he were the type, he certainly wouldn't marry Beth Conroy. She had baggage. He had goals. He was going to be on top again. He was going to win the Finals in October.

He glanced at Beth. She had her face turned up to

the summer sun. He pictured her in that little slip of a nightgown she had on this morning, and thought again of making love to her.

The sun must be cooking his brain.

"You should wear a hat," he told Beth. "The sun'll get to you after a while." Just like it was getting to him.

"This is wonderful. Absolutely wonderful." She leaned over to pat Thunder's neck.

"Glad you're having fun."

"I am."

It did his heart good to see her finally relaxing and not worrying so much. He could tell that she needed a break from everything, especially the demands of caring for a physically challenged child.

He turned his face up to the sun and grinned. This was one benefit of Wheelchair Rodeo he hadn't counted on—and probably neither had Beth.

Following Jake wasn't easy, or maybe it was. Beth couldn't keep her eyes off his backside. His jeans were taut across his butt, and his butt was firmly planted in the saddle. As Lance walked, Jake swayed.

His crisp, checkered shirt was tucked into his jeans as usual. Silver conchos on his brown leather belt glinted in the sun, calling attention to his slim waist.

He was driving her crazy.

She attributed her fascination with him to the fact that she'd been without any kind of male companionship for several years. Even when she was married to Brad, she'd felt alone. Brad had found companionship with his cases of beer and with his pals at work and at the golf course.

Brad had never wanted her to work, claiming "breadwinner" status. It was what he'd wanted, and truthfully she enjoyed puttering. She had never wanted for anything, other than a sober husband and father to Kevin. Her only diversion had been making their house into a showpiece.

"It'll help my career," Brad had insisted. "The house will reflect the fact that I'm well-off and successful, and I'll attract higher caliber clients."

Just as she was about to divorce him, Brad had tried once again to remain sober. After he died and she was sorting through his papers—*their papers*—she discovered thousands of dollars' worth of outstanding bills that a whole battalion of high-caliber stock investors couldn't pay for.

Since he'd never let her take care of the finances, she hadn't known how far beyond their means they were living. It was stupid of her for not insisting that they at least share the financial tasks. It was even more stupid to stay with Brad for as long as she had, but she didn't want to end up like her parents, with seven marriages between them. She'd thought it would be better for Kevin to grow up with both parents, but apparently she'd been wrong.

"How are you doing?" Jake's deep voice was a welcome interruption to her thoughts.

"Wonderful." She inhaled the scent of pine. "It's a beautiful day."

"It sure is." He stopped his horse. "The trail is wide enough for us to walk side by side. I doubt if you want to look at my butt for the whole ride."

If he only knew.

She moved up next to him. "I love how the water

sparkles when the sun shines through the trees and how it makes the water dapple."

He raised an eyebrow. "Dapple?"

"Yes. Dapple." She relaxed her hands that were gripping the reins. "What word would you have used?"

"*Dapple.* Absolutely. I would have used *dapple.*"

She liked his sense of humor, and she liked him more with each hour they spent together.

"Tell me more about Wheelchair Rodeo."

"What do you want to know?"

"How did you come to think of it?"

He swung a leg around the saddle horn to look at her. To him, this slow walk was probably as dull as sitting in a rocking chair. If he wasn't being tossed around like a rag doll for eight seconds on a bull, he was probably bored.

"Ever hear of the Western Wishes program?"

"Sure. It tries to grant the wishes of children who are disabled or fighting illness."

"Exactly. Well, one little gal wanted to meet me. Her name was Chelsea. After a bull-riding in Boise, Idaho, I drove to see her in the hospital. She was just this little thing, and her hair was all gone from chemo, but she had the biggest smile."

"That was nice of you to spare the time, Jake."

He waved off her comment. "She cheated death. She went into remission, and I invited Chelsea and her family to the ranch. I taught her how to ride, and now she's a freshman at UNLV and on the barrel-racing team. She comes every year to help out with Wheelchair Rodeo, but she couldn't make it this year. Her cancer is back."

"Oh, Jake. No. I thought your story was going to have a happy ending."

"I wouldn't count Chelsea out yet. She's a fighter."

"Is she the one whose place I'm taking?"

He nodded. "And we appreciate your help."

"I'll help in whatever way I can, of course! But go on with your story."

"Most of the big events I go to have a little rodeo for disabled kids before the competition. I've always tried to be there to help out. Then it hit me. The Gold Buckle could have a regular program during the summer—you know, expand on what I did with Chelsea. I brought the idea to my folks, and they loved it. My mother added the contest. She thought it would be a break for the caretakers as well as the kids."

Beth straightened her back. "It's a lot of work for you, isn't it? There has to be an enormous amount of organizing and programming."

"It is, but I love to do it. There's something about the look on the kids' faces at the flag raising. They're so excited, so thrilled to be cowboys, if only for a while."

For such a strong man, he was a cream puff. She liked him for that. "For a week, they can forget that they are disabled. That's so important," Beth added. "So, what's tomorrow going to be like?"

"There'll be roping lessons with the cowboys, horses to pick out for the kids who just arrived, lessons on saddling and bridling and horse care. You and Kevin got a jump on that."

He was as excited as Kevin was. She could hear it in his voice.

"After two days of lessons and hands-on, we hit the trail for a campout. That means sleeping under the stars, chuck wagon meals, songs and ghost stories around the campfire, singing and whatever. We have a baseball game, the cowboys against the kids, and there's swimming lessons."

"The kids will love it." Beth remembered that she had volunteered to help out with the girls. "What about bathrooms?"

"Handicapped-accessible and environmentally safe flush toilets. Built by yours truly and some of my buddies a couple years ago."

"Brilliant."

"I know." He grinned at her. "There are two cabins there. My parents use one, the other is the infirmary. They both have all the modern conveniences. There's a picnic pavilion where Cookie sets up his kitchen, and a barn for the horses."

"A cook by the name of Cookie?"

"His real name is Floyd, but all the chuck wagon cooks are traditionally called Cookie."

"How about shower facilities?"

"The river."

"So we sleep in tents?"

"Yep. In sleeping bags."

"Heat?"

"Campfire."

"Snakes?"

"They taste just like chicken."

When she didn't laugh, he added, "Hopefully not," and swung his leg back over into position. "You aren't the camping type?"

"I don't know if I am or not. I've never slept outside or on the ground in my life. Never used a bathroom that wasn't inside and that didn't flush. I don't like toasted marshmallows. Never ate from a chuck wagon. Never knew anyone named Cookie. And until now, I've never been on a horse for any length of time. But I'm willing to give all of it a chance."

"I imagine that's what the pioneers said."

She didn't know if she was a pioneer, but she did feel her spirit returning, and that had everything to do with the cowboy next to her. He was attentive to her. He made her feel attractive. He made her feel alive.

Jake stopped to let her go first over the bridge. She didn't know what made her turn around, but she did.

"What are you looking at, Jake?" She bit back a smile. She knew exactly what he was looking at. The same thing that she'd been looking at on him.

"Thunder, of course," he lied. "Just checking his gait."

"Uh-huh." *So, the cowboy was checking her out.* Interesting. She supposed she should be flattered, but instead it made her jumpy.

They continued along the Chisholm Trail. The front of her cabin was just ahead on the right.

"Home sweet home," she said. She was beginning to feel sore, and her back was killing her.

"No way. You have to unsaddle Thunder, brush him down and clean his tack like every good Wheelchair Rodeo participant."

"You're a tough trail boss."

"You don't know how tough I can be." His gruff act was tempered by the sparkle in his eyes.

"I've read a lot about you, Jake."

"You have?" He raised an eyebrow and grunted. "You've never struck me as a fan."

"When Kevin was in the hospital for one of his operations, he was missing a lot of school and falling behind in his subjects, especially reading. The only things he wanted to read were articles about you. When he wasn't up to reading, he had me read to him. I bought him every bull-riding and cowboy magazine I could. You were in all of them."

Jake looked off at the distant mountains.

"But I never read anything much about Wheelchair Rodeo. Kevin found out about your contest from a letter he received from your fan club. I think we got on a mailing list after I asked them for an autographed picture of you."

He nodded. "I don't talk about Wheelchair Rodeo to the press. We have a steady supply of donations and volunteers and visitors, so I don't need to. I don't want it to seem like I'm using the kids for publicity. The press has a way of tweaking things, and the truth usually gets lost in the translation."

If this cowboy was the real deal, he was one amazing man indeed.

Beth rolled her shoulders. She was getting tired. "Speaking of publicity, I particularly enjoyed watching you rope supermodels on Letterman."

His eyes twinkled. "I enjoyed that, too."

They reached the corral. Their ride on the Chisholm Trail was over. Before they could dismount, Beth reached out and caught Jake's arm.

"The purpose of my telling you about Kevin and his hospital stay was to let you know what you've done to help a little boy get better. Now I can see how you've touched the lives of so many kids. Anyway, I thought you should know." Her eyes filled with tears as she thought of her son enduring one operation after another. "I can see that you run a tight ship here at the Gold Buckle."

He touched his hat brim with his thumb and finger. "Thank you, though I have a feeling that a 'but' is coming."

She tucked her hair behind her ear. "But Kevin is my son and I want to make sure he's okay. I don't want him hurt physically—or emotionally."

"You're more than welcome to watch anytime, but it's not necessary. Our volunteers have been trained, and like you said, I do run a tight ship."

"It's necessary for *me*."

"Is this still about my alleged drinking problem, or are you being protective again?"

She didn't think she was being overprotective, just cautious. She hated drinking. Hated the smell of it. Hated it on someone's breath. Hated to watch how it turned sane people into stupid fools.

"Both." Okay, she'd admit to being overprotective just this once.

A slight frown crossed Jake's face. "Suit yourself." He dismounted and took the reins from her hands before she could say anything else. He gave a quick whistle, and one of the cowboys came running. "Let's get you off of Thunder. Now, just swing your leg over. It's easy. I got you."

When both of Beth's feet hit the dirt, shards of pain shot up her legs. She gasped.

"It'll go away. Just lean on me."

She'd learned never to lean on a man. If she did, she might fall over. But this time she had no choice.

He held her to his side, and she could feel the strength of his arms and the warmth of his chest through her light T-shirt.

Jake handed the reins to a short, thin cowboy with a shiny face and freckles. "Would you mind taking care of the horses for us, Will?"

"Be glad to," said the cowboy as he led the horses away.

"This time I'm going to forget my rules about taking care of your own horse," he said.

"I can pull my weight. Just give me a minute to find my legs."

"Don't worry about it." He pointed to a group of kids by the bunkhouse. "Do you see Kevin over there?"

"Of course I do." He was the first person she had looked for when she rode in.

"No. Really look at him, Beth. Tell me what you see."

"Kevin is sitting in his wheelchair and watching a cowboy show him how to rope a plastic steer head that is stuck into a bale of hay."

"But how does he *look?*" Jake pushed.

"He looks happier than I've ever seen him. He looks like a ten year old should. He has kids around him who are in wheelchairs like he is. He's making friends, branching out, and he's mesmerized by the cowboy who's twirling a rope over his head."

"That's Jason Wyatt doing the teaching. He has five kids of his own. He comes from a big, extended ranch-family with lots of nieces and nephews. I'd say he knows his way around kids like he knows his way around bulls."

"Kevin's having fun."

"Fun? That's part of it. He's fingering a rope. Dying to try it himself. But what I'm getting at is that you were gone for a while and he's perfectly okay. You can have some time to yourself without worrying about Kevin so much."

She stepped away. Her legs were working again. "Tell me, Jake, how would you feel if you saw your child all broken and bleeding?"

He winced. That question hit him right in the gut. He didn't want to see any kids like that. Kids were cute and fun and trusting, and he hated to see them hurt or suffering. "Kevin was barely conscious in the ambulance after the accident. I held his hand, and I wouldn't let it go until they pried me away. With every breath I drew, I willed him to live. Otherwise I couldn't have gone on living or breathing myself."

"I'd feel the same way," Jake said softly.

"Can you understand, then, why I protect him? Why I keep him close by my side and fuss over him? Why I give him everything I possibly can in the world?"

"That's why you brought him here," Jake said. It was a statement, not a question.

"Yes. That's why I brought him here."

"Then why don't you let him have some fun? And while you're at it, let *yourself* have some fun."

"You don't understand."

"You're still punishing yourself. You won't allow yourself to have fun because you feel you don't deserve it. I see it all the time with parents who come here."

A major curse word was on the tip of her tongue, but she held it back. Her hands balled into fists, and she pressed them to her sides in case she was tempted to let them fly into his jaw.

But how could she, when deep down inside she knew that the cowboy was absolutely correct? Still, however good his intentions, his criticism cut deep.

"Beth, I'm sorry. Like you said before, I have no right."

She held a hand up for him to stop. "Seems like all we do is apologize to each other. Maybe we should just keep our distance."

Chapter Five

"I'm an idiot," Jake mumbled as he mucked out Thunder's stall. "A complete jackass. Why the hell am I getting involved with guests? Why her?"

He nudged Lance's rump out of the way and chucked a pitchfork full of matted hay into a wheelbarrow. Lance pushed him in the back with his nose, and Jake almost fell in the stuff.

"I'm not in the mood, Lance."

He wheeled the load out and closed the stall. Then Jake spotted him—Clint Scully, the best rodeo clown in the business.

Clint yawned from his cocoon in the fresh hay. "Can't a guy get any sleep in this outfit?" He extended his hand.

Jake took Clint's hand and pulled him out of the loose hay. "Is the bunkhouse too modern for you?"

"Too much noise." Clint gave another big yawn, then stuck the end of a blade of hay into his mouth. "What's up?"

"What makes you think that anything is up?"

"I've known you long enough to know that when you're talking to yourself and mucking stalls like you're mining the mother lode, you're bothered about something. Now, if it ain't something to do with bull riding, it has to be a woman. So which one is it?"

"None of your business."

"Tell Uncle Clint. I can help."

"You're not my uncle, and you have enough woman trouble of your own."

Clint sat down on a folding chair. "Ah, so it *is* a woman that has your jeans in a knot?"

"Yeah."

"Let's go to the Last Chance tonight and you can cry in your beer."

"Can't do it, Clint. I got a million things to do before tomorrow. And I could use your help."

Clint brushed some hay off his sleeves. "That's why I'm here. Since you've just changed the subject, I'll assume you want me to mind my own business."

"You got it."

"Then give me something to do."

Jake handed him the mucking rake. "How about finishing this while I go pick some apology wildflowers for a lady."

Clint slapped a hand on his heart. "Picking flowers? Shoot. You got it bad, you know that?"

"Ya' think?"

"Yup."

* * *

You won't allow yourself to have fun because you think you don't deserve it.

Beth wasn't really concentrating on the roping instruction. She was enjoying the company of Kevin and the other kids who had arrived early, but Jake's words kept running through her mind.

When it was Kevin's turn to give it a try, he circled the official Jake Dixon rope over his head and let it loose. He lassoed the horns on the plastic steer head and pulled the rope taut.

Beth let out a cheer, but Kevin didn't seem to hear. He was too busy high-fiveing the cowboys and the other kids.

Inez, the owner of the apartment complex where she worked, once said that after children are born it's the responsibility of the parents to start preparing them to leave the nest. "Just like the birds, Beth. Just like the birds," she'd said.

But her little bird was broken and scarred from too many operations: his femur, his pelvis, his collarbone, discs…

She couldn't push him out of the nest, so to speak. But she could give him more space to spread his wings.

Darn that Jake Dixon. He might be right.

She walked over to Kevin, leaned over and whispered that she was going to grab a bite to eat in the mess hall. "Would you like to join me?"

He looked around her at the next roper. "No way, Mom. This is so awesome." When he made eye contact with her, he explained, "I want to eat with the other kids and the cowboys. Okay?"

"That's fine, Kevin. You have a good time."

"We'll see that he gets something to eat, ma'am," said a cowboy twirling a rope over his head. "Cookie's putting on some hot dogs and hamburgers and a big pot of beans."

"Did you hear that, Mom? Beans!"

A bean had never crossed Kevin's lips.

She ruffled his hair and immediately regretted it when she heard a snicker from the boy sitting next to him. She noticed the embarrassed flush on his cheeks as he smoothed his hair back down.

"See ya' later, Mom."

"Have a great time," she said, but Kevin's attention was on another cowboy who was demonstrating "wrist action."

Beth walked to her cabin to freshen up. When she climbed the stairs to the porch, a flash of color caught her eye. On one of the rocking chairs was a bouquet of wildflowers. She froze as unhappy memories flooded her.

Brad had given her flowers all the time. Flowers when he didn't show up for dinner, when he forgot Kevin's games because he was at a bar, whenever they fought over his drinking…

She picked these flowers up and inhaled their fragrance. They were a colorful mix that she didn't recognize. There were yellows and purples, and some white Queen Anne's Lace.

Were they from Jake?

Maybe they were his way of apologizing for his earlier unsolicited advice.

She smiled as she inhaled again. They weren't fancy

flowers from a shop, but they held more meaning for her. Jake had picked them himself; he hadn't simply picked up a phone and ordered them. Not that he could. There probably wasn't a flower shop within two hundred miles of here.

She put them in a glass and filled it with water. Then she placed it on the kitchen table. They looked perfect in the rustic cabin.

Then she did another thing she hadn't done in years—a luxury that she never allowed herself. She went back on the porch, plopped herself in the hammock and closed her eyes.

She was going to take a nap in the middle of the afternoon.

Three hours later, she woke to the squeak of Kevin's wheelchair coming up the ramp.

"Are you okay, Mom?"

She yawned and wiped at her eyes. "I'm fine. Why?"

"You're sleeping in the middle of the day."

"It must be the fresh air."

"You're not sick?"

"I'm just fine." And she was. The nap had been just what she'd needed.

"We're supposed to meet Jake over at the mess hall for supper. Hear that, Mom? We're going to eat supper with Jake Dixon."

If Kevin were any happier, he'd burst. She didn't have the heart to tell him that she'd rather not and that she'd decided to keep her distance from the amateur cowboy-psychiatrist. If she wanted analysis, she'd go to a professional.

She took a deep breath and put a smile on her face. "Dinner with Jake would be fine, Kevin. About what time?"

"He said six o'clock."

It was five-thirty now. "I'll get ready and you get washed up. How did the roping go?"

"K.C. told me that I was the best."

She stopped herself from ruffling his hair. "Cool."

"And I had hot dogs and beans. The beans were heated up from a can."

"Imagine that!"

It didn't take her long to run a comb through her hair, wash her face and put on a little makeup. Dressing up wasn't necessary. No one wore anything but jeans at the Gold Buckle.

It took Kevin a little longer, but when he came out of the bathroom, he was freshly scrubbed and he smelled like spices. He had a few more golden freckles across his nose from the sun.

She sniffed the air. "What's that you have on, Kevin?"

"Ramon gave it to all of us cowboys. It's called Bull-istic. The people who make it are one of Ramon's sponsors. He gave the girls perfume called Yellow Rose too." He reached into the pouch that hung from his wheelchair and handed her a little box. "I asked Ramon for one for you."

"Why, how nice. Thanks for thinking of me, sweetie."

"Sure."

She dabbed a little perfume on her wrists. "Mmm…smells good." It had a musky rose scent.

"Hey, Mom?"

"Yes?"

"Do you like Jake?" His eyes were hopeful.

"Why…yes, sure. He's a nice man. Why do you ask?" She took a deep breath.

"I was just wondering."

"Honey, he's a nice man. That's all."

Kevin's face showed exactly what he had on his mind—hope that Jake Dixon would be more to them than a "nice man."

"Let's go eat, okay?" she said.

"Mom, I forgot to tell you that I get to move into the bunkhouse with the other kids tonight. Isn't that cool?"

"Very cool, Kevin." But her heart sank. Would he really be safe there?

"You'll be all alone," he said, a touch of concern in his expression.

Beth shrugged off her fears and smiled. "Don't worry about me. I'll be just fine."

"You sure?"

"I'm absolutely sure."

That perked him up. Then she saw that although his eyes were bright, they were a little droopy. "You've had a long day. Let me push your wheelchair to dinner. I had a nice, long nap, so I'm wide awake."

"Naw, I'll do it. I don't want anyone to think I'm a wimp."

Beth walked slowly beside Kevin. When they got to the mess hall, a slim cowboy with a huge spongy orange cowboy hat perched on his head was leading a sing-along to "Home on the Range."

Pots clanged, dishes and glasses tinkled, laughter

rang out. Beth and Kevin dodged wheelchairs, crutches and pedestrians and made their way to an empty table.

"Mom, there's Clint Scully! And J.C.! And Ross and Justin! Oh, there's Gilbert and Adam! And here comes Jake!"

They all looked familiar from TV and she'd read about them, but she didn't recognize them the way Kevin did. She did see Jake making his way through the crowd to their table. Along the way, he stopped and talked. He shook hands with the kids and sometimes he crouched down to get eye-to-eye with them. There was always pain etched on his face when he tried to get back up.

He had changed into a dark pair of jeans, or else they were brand new and never washed. He wore a dark green shirt with long sleeves with some kind of logo on it. Sponsor advertising, she guessed.

He seemed inches taller than everyone else, or maybe it was just his presence that commanded attention. Whatever it was, Beth couldn't take her eyes off him.

"Howdy, Kev!" He shook hands with him, then tweaked his hat to her. "How are you doing, Beth?"

"Fine. Do I have you to thank for the flowers?"

He nodded. "Apology accepted?"

"Accepted."

"Good. Shall we get some grub?"

He put his hand on the small of her back, directing her to the line. Then he picked up a red plastic tray and handed one to her and one to Kevin. As they moved their trays along, they helped themselves to fried chicken, mashed potatoes and a tossed green salad.

Kevin kept up his endless chatter, so it was easy for her to sit back and watch Jake Dixon. She loved how he related to Kevin and never talked down to her son. Several cowboys, kids and parents stopped by to talk to Jake. He was gracious to everyone, and she could tell they all adored him.

Although she continued to recognize several of the cowboys when Jake introduced her, Kevin knew their stats, their current ranking for the Finals, their injuries and their ninety-point rides. Kevin couldn't be happier, and that did her heart good. This was just what she'd hoped for.

After eating what he could between interruptions, Jake excused himself to make an announcement. With his long, uneven strides that she had come to recognize, she watched as he climbed the two steps to the raised platform. She waited for the pain to appear on his face, and it did.

"Welcome, everyone, to the annual Gold Buckle Wheelchair Rodeo." Jake took his hat off and waved it in the air. "We are going to have a great time!"

His enthusiasm was contagious. There was hooting and hollering and hat tossing. The cowboys were getting the kids excited, and the kids got right into it.

"After dinner, the Wheelchair Rodeo participants will move into the bunkhouses. The bunkhouse with the blue door is for the cowboys, and the one with the pink door is for the cowgirls."

There was more hand clapping and hooting.

"The program will begin at eight o'clock in the morning with the Pledge of Allegiance and a nondenominational cowboy and cowgirl prayer at the flagpole. Family and friends are welcome. A schedule of each day's events will be available on your way out. In two days, the overnight trail ride will begin. This will be followed by Wheelchair Rodeo, where prizes will be given in each event." He paused. "And that means Gold Buckles!"

There was pounding on the tables, whistling and several yee-haws. The kids were in a frenzy, as excited as they could be. Their faces were flushed, their bodies were wiggling and a few wheelchairs spun in circles. Kevin was no exception. He was ready to rocket out of his wheelchair.

"Now my mother, Mrs. Emily Dixon, would like to say a few words."

When Jake came down from the platform and walked back toward Beth, his limp was even more pronounced.

As he sat down, his shoulder brushed hers, and when he reached for the hot sauce at the same time as she reached for a napkin, their fingers touched. A rush of heat coursed through her when he smiled.

She tried to listen to Emily's words, but Jake was too distracting. His Bull-istic aftershave drifted her way when he leaned over to say something to Kevin. Taking a deep breath, she committed the scent to memory.

Her mouth was dry, and she felt like a high school freshman with a crush. She reached for her iced tea and drank what was left in one gulp. She chewed on the remaining ice cubes, although she wanted to drop them in her bra or press them to her forehead to cool herself down.

Jake stood up after Emily was done with her speech

and everyone started moving out. "I'll walk you two back to your cabin and help move Kevin's gear into the bunkhouse."

"Thank you," Beth said.

She felt his hand, hot on her back, as he guided her through the crowd leaving the hall. As they walked to her cabin, she was grateful for the crisp air. It was helping her cool off.

The *thud-thud* of Jake's boots on the gravel made her smile. All that was needed was the twinkle of spurs and a Colt dangling from each hip, and they could be walking down the main street of a small Western town in 1880.

A little later, as she was gathering Kevin's gear and putting it in his saddle bag, it hit her that she'd be alone at the cabin.

She felt giddy—and guilty—at the thought. It'd been a long time since she'd been free of responsibility, free to do anything she wanted during the next day.

So take that, Jake Dixon. Maybe there was hope for her yet.

She walked back into the living room and Jake took the bag from her.

"Don't worry about Kevin. He'll be fine. But how about you? Are you going to be okay here alone?"

Alone. There had been many times that she'd been alone in her marriage, even when Brad was there. But she wasn't thinking of Brad. She was thinking of Jake.

She pictured Jake stretched out naked on her bed. His hat was on the bedpost. His boots and jeans were in a pile on the floor. His blue eyes were dark with passion. She was wearing her buy-one-get-one-free red nightgown from Wal-Mart. He'd hold out his hand, much as he was doing now, and he'd say…

"Beth, are you okay?" He shook her hand. "We'll take good care of Kev. *I promise.*" He stressed the last two words. "See you at the flagpole at eight a.m. sharp."

She took a deep breath and exhaled, letting her daydream vanish. "'Night. I will hold you to your promise, Jake."

He touched his hat. "Good night."

She leaned over to give Kevin a kiss, but she saw his eyes dart to Jake and back to her. She got the message: He wasn't a kid.

She held out her hand to shake his. "Good night, cowboy."

He shook her hand. "'Night, Mom."

Jake winked at her, and it loosened the lump in her throat. Her little boy was growing up.

"Have a good time," she said.

"I sure will," Kevin said. "Let's go, Jake!"

She watched from the porch as Kevin wheeled and Jake walked next to him. Jake had laid a hand on Kevin's shoulder and, silhouetted in the moonlight, they almost looked like father and son.

If only things had been different. If only Brad had not been an alcoholic. If only she'd known that he'd relapsed. If only there hadn't been that awful accident.

If only she could be sure Jake Dixon didn't drink.

If only she didn't like Jake Dixon so much.

That admission shocked her, and she filed it in the back of her mind. She didn't want another man in her life, especially another man who might have a drinking problem.

An hour later, as she was reading a magazine, she realized that she'd forgotten to pick up a program from the mess hall. Out of habit, she was about to tell Kevin where she was going, but then she remembered that he wasn't there.

She stepped into her shoes and walked down the path back to the mess hall. As she passed the corral, she saw Jake talking to his father. In one of Jake's hands was a clipboard that he was looking at under the glow of an overhead light. In his other hand was a bottle of beer.

He lifted the beer to his lips and took a long draw.

Her stomach lurched and a shiver of dread crawled up her spine. Beth kept to the shadows and took the long way back to her cabin, past the boys' bunkhouse.

Her guard was back in place.

Eight o'clock in the morning came mighty early for Jake, since he didn't get to bed until about two.

He had some minor details to work out on both Wheelchair Rodeo and the Challenge, but he was convinced that with a couple of phone calls, he could concentrate on Wheelchair Rodeo.

He stood in the shower of the ranch house, letting the hot water sluice over him. Maybe it would help his leg and his back and everything else that was aching.

Mentally, he geared up for the days ahead. There were thirty kids this year and about the same number of cowboys and volunteers. The majority of kids couldn't ride a horse. On the campout, those kids would ride in a couple of hay wagons in their wheelchairs. Other kids, like Kevin, who had the consent of his physician, were okayed to ride on the special saddles he had had custom made with back and side support and safety belts.

It all required a great deal of training, medical releases, alertness, and a lot of doctors on staff along with EMTs, nurses, cowboys and other volunteers who donated their time. In exchange, he made sure that everyone got front-row seats to the Gold Buckle Challenge.

Since Beth was a volunteer, she'd be there with Kevin. He liked the fact that she'd see Jake ride in the Challenge.

But he'd be riding against his doctor's advice. Dr. Mike Trotter had told him that it wasn't a good idea—that he should sit it out so he didn't get injured even worse. But he had to ride at his own event, for heaven's sake. So he was going to ignore Trot and cowboy up.

He dressed in a hurry and entered the kitchen, where his mother handed him a cup of steaming coffee. His father nodded at him over the newspaper.

"Ready for another year, Jake?" Emily asked.

"Ready as I'll ever be. How about you both?"

"All set," Dex Dixon said.

Emily wiped the kitchen table. When the sponge came near Dex, he lifted the paper, the way Jake had seen him do hundreds of times before. What would it be like to be that in tune with another human being?

"Maybe there is one thing you can do," Emily began.

Jake immediately grabbed his clipboard and a pen to write it down. "What's that, Mom?"

"I think that Beth Conroy needs to go out and have some fun. Why don't you take her dancing?" Before

Jake could respond, she turned to Dex. "Don't you think so, dear?"

Dex lowered the paper so that only his eyes were showing. "Sounds like a good idea to me, Em."

Jake slid his clipboard onto the counter and crossed his arms. "If this isn't a setup, I don't know what is. You two have to stop your matchmaking. Just because you had a couple successes with Cousin Laurie and Harry at the feed store and Betty Summerville and Rich O'Brien—"

"Don't forget Miss Spader, the librarian, and Delbert Montrain," Em added.

"The jury's still out on that one, Em," Dex said.

Jake shook his head. "Beth Conroy and I don't have a thing in common. Besides, I'm too busy with Wheelchair Rodeo."

"Son, you have it organized inside and out. Your mother and I can keep an eye on things tonight. You go out and have a little fun."

"Dad, it's my responsibility."

Dex waved him away. "We've all agreed to share the responsibility. Now, go ask that little gal out and kick up your heels."

"And," Em added, "don't forget that she's a contest winner. We owe it to her to show her a good time."

"I agree with your mother. Both of you certainly could use a good time."

Em laid a hand on Jake's arm. "After the campfire, the kids will be going to bed. We have more than enough volunteers, and most of them are well-trained veterans of the last two WRs. There's nothing that we can't handle."

No sense arguing with them, and he wasn't about to tell them that he'd already thought about asking Beth out. That would just encourage them. "Okay. I'll take her out. If I don't, I'll never hear the end of it from you two."

"Fine." Dex got up from his seat at the table and looked at his watch. "Let's go. We don't want to be late for the opening."

As Jake tucked his shirt into his jeans, they walked out to the flagpole. His mother would lead the Pledge of Allegiance. After that, his father would read his Cowboy/Cowgirl Prayer. He had written it for the first Wheelchair Rodeo three years ago, and reading it was now a tradition.

Jake scanned the crowd for Beth. He spotted her standing off to the side, not by Kevin. Maybe what he'd said about giving the kid some space had actually struck a chord with her. She had on a dark pair of jeans that looked new and a pretty blue T-shirt. Her hair looked like spun gold in the morning sun.

He knew the exact second she spotted him. Her mouth thinned into a tight line and she looked away. What the hell had he done now? Thinking back to last night, he remembered leaving her cabin on good terms.

The woman could be as prickly as a cactus—but there was something about her… She was both tough and vulnerable. It would have been easy for her to crumble when her husband died and Kevin was injured, but she was a fighter.

He'd made it a point to read Kevin's file. "I want my mother to have a vacation because she looks tired all the time and she worries too much," the boy had written. That little bit said a lot.

Maybe she did need a night on the town and a little Jake Dixon charm.

He decided to ask her out. They'd drive over to the Last Chance Saloon on the outskirts of Mountain Springs. They'd do a little boot scootin', have a few laughs and a couple of drinks.

Yes. That's just what Beth Conroy needed.

He looked tired.

Or hungover.

Or both.

Beth glanced over at Jake. He had dark shadows under his eyes and there was a slight slump to his shoulders. He stifled a yawn.

Last night, she had been tempted to go storming over to the boys' bunkhouse, pound on the blue door and wheel her son right out of the place.

But when she'd glanced through the window, the kids had been gathered in a circle and a couple of cowboys were telling stories.

So she'd backed off.

Looking away from him, she listened as one of the kids played an off-key trumpet. K.C. and Ramon raised the flag. Emily Dixon led everyone in the Pledge of Allegiance.

Then it was Dexter Dixon's turn to speak.

"As sure as the sun rises and sets each day
And the mountains stand strong
We will try to do our best.
Not just now, but every day of our lives.
That's the cowboy and the cowgirl way."

There was a moment of silence and then Dex Dixon shouted, "Welcome, contestants and volunteers, to Wheelchair Rodeo!"

Beth hooted and yelled with everyone. She was just wishing she had a cowboy hat to throw in the air like everyone else, when one suddenly appeared in her hands.

"Thought you'd like it," Jake said.

The deep voice, the unique scent, the blue eyes with the laugh lines, the thin scars on his face, the complex cowboy who thought to bring her a hat—this was the package that was Jake Dixon. He had the power to get her blood boiling with one sentence.

"Try it on."

It fit perfectly. "A white hat must mean I'm a good guy."

"Are you?" Jake asked.

"Absolutely."

He shrugged and grinned. "Too bad."

Her breath caught. "Yes. Too bad." For just once, she'd like to throw caution to the wind and do something totally out of character, maybe even with Jake Dixon.

"It was one of the first hats I won at a small rodeo in Kaycee back when I was in high school. It was too small for me, but it fits you perfectly. It's yours."

"Thank you" was all she managed to say before Clint Scully grabbed Jake's arm and asked him a question.

Cowboys with clipboards began dividing the kids into groups. Kevin wheeled away without a goodbye.

"Well, I'd better get moving," Jake said, looking back at Beth. "What do you have planned for the day?"

"I'll watch the program a bit, but first, I'm going to join the crowd at the mess hall and have some coffee. Then there's a book calling me that I borrowed from the lobby library. I'm looking forward to rocking on my porch and reading it."

"How about going dancing with me tonight?"

His question took her by surprise. It seemed like a lifetime ago that she'd last danced.

"Kevin'll be fine. There's a bonfire tonight and a sing-along. There'll be plenty of marshmallows along with plenty of supervision."

"I-I—" It was on the tip of her tongue to decline, but she couldn't get the words out.

"Nothing fancy. Just jeans. How about eight o'clock? I'll be free by then."

She didn't answer.

"Great! I'll pick you up at your cabin."

Before she could catch her breath, he was halfway to the corral.

"Why didn't I say no?" she mumbled, but she knew the reason.

She *wanted* to go.

Chapter Six

Beth had planned only to have coffee at the dining hall, but Cookie insisted that she needed "fattening up" and handed her a dish heaped with home fries, scrambled eggs, bacon and a slab of ham. He was a beanpole of a man who obviously didn't eat his own cooking.

What could she do? Cookie had obviously never heard that greaseless cooking was a good thing.

She found a newspaper at one of the tables and sat down with her red plastic tray. Taking a sip of coffee, she opened the *Wyoming Angler* and read about how the trout were biting at Absaraka Lake and the best bait were night crawlers and salmon eggs. Ick.

She was reading that for catching catfish the angler should do something with chicken liver, when Emily Dixon pulled up a chair across from her.

"How are you doing, Beth? Having fun?"

"I am. It's a wonderful place. And I've never had so much time alone. It takes getting used to."

"And Kevin?"

"He's in his cowboy glory. I can't thank you enough for picking us to win your contest. A week here is just what we needed. My cabin is so homey, and I love the mountains and the horses and the fresh air—just everything."

"Dex and I love every square inch of this ranch. So does Jake, but he doesn't spend a lot of time here, with all the traveling he does. My other boys are busy going off in other directions. Jake's our only hope to take over the ranch."

Beth swallowed a mouthful of eggs. "How many other sons do you have?"

"Ty is in vet school at Cornell University in New York. Cody can't decide if he's going to be the next Alan Jackson or a social worker, so mostly he's a professional student. He's at Texas A&M, probably changing his major as we speak." Em clasped her hands together. "I have a daughter, too. Karen. She's going to the University of Nevada at Las Vegas. Our Karen has always enjoyed the big-city lights and excitement."

"And Jake's the bull rider," Beth said. "He never went to college?"

"The ink wasn't dry yet on his high school diploma when he went on the road to follow the rodeos, but he has excellent business sense and a way with animals and children."

"Yes, he does," Beth said.

"All the women chase after him, too, but no one's

struck his interest. Until you." Emily's eyes twinkled. "I hear you're going dancing tonight."

Beth's mouth hung open like a trout in Absaraka Lake anticipating a night crawler or a salmon egg.

"He wanted to take you dancing something fierce, so of course, Dex and I volunteered to watch things here."

"That's…really nice of you." Beth was at a loss for words.

"Jake's a good man, Beth. He's just been dealt a couple of bad hands lately."

"He seems to be a good man, but…" She didn't want to question his mother about his drinking problem, nor the half-dozen other worries she had about getting close to him.

"But?"

She hesitated. "But I'm not looking to get involved. Not with Jake. Not with anyone." Beth toyed with the fried potatoes on her plate.

"No one's asking you to get involved." Emily patted her hand. "You just go and have fun on your date. Everyone will keep an eye on Kevin."

Her heart fluttered. *Date?* She hadn't considered that she was going on a *date.* That put a whole different light on things.

A volunteer with "EMT" on her name tag approached their table, requesting Emily's attention on a supply matter. They both said their goodbye's and hurried off. Beth was alone again, glad she didn't have to think about Jake or dates or anything else.

She took a bite of ham, speared some fried potatoes, picked up the *Wyoming Angler* and read about using worm harnesses to catch walleyes.

* * *

To work off her cholesterol-laden breakfast, Beth decided to take a walk around the grounds. She found herself drawn to the corral and the horses gathered in the shade of the barn.

A petite woman with short red hair and freckles came over and introduced herself. Maggie told her that her daughter was in the Wheelchair Rodeo program and was just about to have a riding lesson in the corral.

"My son Kevin's in it too. It's a great program."

"It definitely is. Heather couldn't talk about anything else for months."

"Kevin was the same."

They were talking more about their kids when suddenly, a young girl about Kevin's age flew out of the barn, wheeling frantically into the corral. Long red hair streamed out behind her and she sobbed to the point of hiccups.

Maggie grabbed the top rail of the fence and yelled. "Heather! Heather Ann, what are you doing?"

There were horses in the corral and, tame or not, it wasn't good for Heather to be there alone. As Beth and Maggie began to climb the corral fence to rescue the girl, Beth noticed two cowboys rushing toward Heather. Jake appeared from nowhere and began walking toward the girl. He waved the volunteers away.

Beth put a hand on Maggie's arm. "Wait a second. Let's see how Jake handles this."

Heather stopped wheeling as Jake called her name. Struggling on the uneven ground, he finally reached her. He knelt on one knee, his hand reaching out to steady himself on the arm of Heather's chair.

"What's wrong, honey?"

She tried to talk, but all she could do was hiccup.

"I have to go to her," Maggie insisted.

"Trust me. Just wait."

Maggie reminded Beth of herself. A few days ago—yesterday even—she would have flown over the fence and run to Kevin. Now she was the one telling this young mother to wait before intervening?

Jake pulled a red bandana from his pocket and handed it to the girl. "So what's the problem?" Jake asked Heather. "It can't be as bad as all that."

"I don't like my horse." Heather sniffed. "I was too late to get the horse that I really want. That horse was taken."

"What horse do you have now?"

"Smoke. He's a boring gray. I want the beautiful golden one."

"Smoke's real name is Smoke Signal. He's the great-great-grandson—actually I don't know how many greats—of a horse that was owned by an Indian warrior. A real Indian princess loaned Smoke to Wheelchair Rodeo. Did you know that?"

The small hitch in her shoulders ceased as her eyes grew as wide as saucers. "Really?"

"Really." Jake nodded. "Her Indian name is Gentle Fawn, and she doesn't let just anyone ride Smoke. They have to be really special. Just like you."

"Really? Wow!" She wiped her wet face with the bandana. "Can I meet Gentle Fawn?"

"You've met her already. She's the bunkhouse nurse, Fawn Murray."

"Fawn's a real Indian princess?"

"She sure is. Ask her. Now, let me see about getting you that palomino."

"No! Um…uh, I think I'd like to keep Smoke Signal after all."

"Are you sure?"

"Yes."

"Okay. Now, do you think you can help me up?"

Heather laughed as Jake clowned around trying to stand from his squat position. But having seen him limp often in the past couple of days, Beth knew he probably *couldn't* get up easily. She wanted to help him herself, but knew it was better for his ego if she just stayed in the shadows.

Jake finally stood, paused to take some deep breaths and rubbed his leg. Then he wheeled Heather into the barn.

"Do you think that story about the Indian princess and all is true?" Maggie asked Beth.

"Well, Fawn Murray is a nurse in the girls' bunkhouse. I've met her."

"You know, Beth, Jake's really wonderful with kids." Maggie sighed. "And the man is gorgeous."

"Yes," said Beth. "Yes, he is."

For the rest of the day, she couldn't get Jake out of her mind or out of her vision. No matter where she went, he seemed to be nearby with a riding class, a roping class, or sitting on a bale of hay flipping papers over his clipboard.

Later, while she was on her porch reading, a riding class, led by Jake, came off the Chisholm Trail.

She admired how he looked at one with the horse.

There was no question that Jake Dixon was a real cowboy. He wore the traditional boots and hat and the clothes, but there was something more. Not only did he look at home in the saddle, he looked like part of this rugged place.

He waved as he rode by. "Hey, how about saddling up Thunder and joining the next class in a half hour? We're riding the Santa Fe Trail. You could use more practice for the overnight trail ride."

"Sure." She put a bookmark in her place. She could have hurried inside, but she took the opportunity to watch him ride away….

Then she dashed inside to get her cowboy hat and to put on some makeup. She never wore the stuff when she wasn't working, but today she would.

It wasn't just being with Jake that made her eager. She welcomed the opportunity to ride Thunder again. Hurrying into the barn, she grabbed a carrot from the bin in front. She stopped at Thunder's stall and fed it to him, then ran a hand over the velvety softness of his neck.

"We're going for a ride, Thunder."

The horse nodded his great head as if he understood.

"I'm going to saddle you, and I'd appreciate if you'd help me out."

Thunder shook his head from side to side.

"Aww…come on."

She saw his saddle blanket on a rack. Easy. After getting the saddle, she heaved it up on his back.

"Now, don't blow yourself up. I don't want to push my knee against your belly. Promise me."

The horse didn't move.

She set up the cinch and tightened it with all her strength.

"Thanks. Now the bridle." She pulled it from the hook.

He let her put it on without a problem.

She took in a deep breath and let it out. "I think we're all set now."

Her nerves were jumping with excitement. She was going to ride, and she was going to ride with Jake. She liked his company, but she wasn't sure about her date with him. That was too…well…intimate.

She heard a sharp whistle and took it as a signal that the Santa Fe Trail ride was starting. Leading Thunder out of the barn, she joined the others.

"Is he cinched tight?" Jake asked. "You don't want to fall off, saddle and all."

"As tight as I can get it."

"I'll check it."

He started to get down from his horse, but she waved him back. She didn't want him to exert himself. "No. It's fine. Really."

Jake nodded. "Mount up, then."

It took her four tries of hopping on one foot to get into the saddle. When she did, she gave a thumbs-up sign. The Wheelchair Rodeo kids applauded.

Jake returned her thumbs-up, then motioned with a jerk of his head for her to fall in line next to him.

He gave her a wink as she joined him. "We'll be riding drag."

She must have looked puzzled, so he added, "At the end of the line. I want to keep a good eye on the kids."

"Is everyone ready?" He held his arm up as if he was making a right turn.

"Ready, boss!"

K.C. was leading the ride. A young cowboy she'd met at the chuck hall last night by the name of Troy was positioned in the middle.

"Are the Wheelchair Rodeo riders ready?" Jake shouted.

"Yeah!"

"Then let's ride," Jake said, pointing his finger at the woods straight ahead.

As K.C. nudged his horse forward, the rest of the horses fell in line.

After they were under way, Jake turned to Beth. "When I saw you reading on the porch, I remembered that I wanted you to get some more practice in. Kevin's all set. He rode this morning and right now he's roping. He's a great little roper. I think he's going to win the competition."

She already knew exactly what Kevin was doing, but it was nice of Jake to let her know that Kevin was okay.

"Hope I didn't disturb your plans for the day," he said.

"No. Not at all. I was hoping for the chance to ride again."

"Then you'll like the Santa Fe Trail. It goes through the woods and the prettiest meadow that you've ever seen."

"Sounds wonderful."

She took a deep breath. Whenever she smelled pine from now on, she'd always think of the Gold Buckle Ranch and riding Thunder. She'd think of Jake Dixon too.

"Jake?"

"Yes?"

"I saw you with Heather Ann. You were wonderful with her."

"It was nothing."

"It was everything. You made her feel special."

Her eyes met his, and he smiled.

Then those blue eyes twinkled with mischief. "Why, Beth, be careful. I might think you're starting to like me."

She chuckled. "Heather loved your Indian princess story."

"It was rather brilliant, wasn't it?"

"Sure was. Is it true?"

"A cowboy never lies."

She laughed. "Is that part of the cowboy code of honor?"

"It's Jake Dixon's code of honor."

Beth liked that. Jake didn't lie, and he was wonderful with kids—two admirable traits. He was also kind to animals and looked great in jeans. What more could a woman want?

They rode in silence, comfortable with each other. Beth enjoyed the chirping of the birds and the *clip-clop* of the horses' hooves on the path. The kids were chattering happily but she was able to block them out and just take pleasure in the scenery—and the man next to her.

Soon they broke out of the cool of the woods into a meadow of wildflowers. The transition took her breath away. The breeze moved the flowers and the tall shiny grass in an undulating rhythm. It was much warmer here, and the scent of flowers permeated the air. She recognized some of the flowers from the bouquet that Jake had given her.

"I wish this could be bottled into perfume. I'd always wear it."

"And I'd always move close to you so I could smell it."

She laughed. Jake had a way of making her laugh—the way Brad used to when they were just married, but that was a long time ago. In recent years, she couldn't remember a time when she'd laughed as much as she had on this trip.

But she had to stop comparing Jake to Brad— even though Brad was her only point of reference.

Beth leaned over in the saddle to look at a monarch butterfly sitting on a lacy, white flower and suddenly found herself flying sideways through the air, the flower and the butterfly rising up to meet her.

She gave an unladylike grunt when she landed on the ground, saddle and all, right on top of her hat. She hoped the butterfly had escaped death. The kids laughed.

Thunder nudged her with his nose, then dipped his head to graze.

Jake dismounted and was by her side as fast as he could manage. He winced as he knelt down next to her. He was probably in more pain than she was.

"Are you hurt?"

"Only my pride."

He moved the saddle off her as if it were a toy, not thirty-five pounds of leather and whatever. He picked up her hat. It looked like a lopsided dinner plate.

"K.C, move 'em out. Troy, you take drag. We'll catch up."

"Okay, boss," K.C. said as Troy took position.

Jake knelt down next to her as she lay in the wildflowers. His hands moved up and down her legs, checking for broken bones.

She took a deep breath. His touch was gentle yet firm, sending tiny waves of pleasure through her.

"Jake, I'm fine. Let me up."

As he changed position, she could see how he was hurting by the pain etched on his face.

"Let me check your arms for broken bones."

He was so close. So close that she could see several tiny scars on his face. She couldn't resist reaching up and touching one just below his eye.

Jake stopped and stared at her.

"Where did you get this?" she asked, not moving her finger.

"Colorado Springs."

She could feel his breath on her face as he studied her, looked intently into her eyes as if he were thinking…wondering…

She knew what he was going to do, knew she should stop it before it started—but she couldn't. *Only this once,* she told herself. Maybe then she'd stop dreaming about him, stop fantasizing about him, stop wanting to touch him.

Just this once.

Lowering his head, Jake touched his lips to hers. It was tentative at first, as if he was testing her, wondering if she'd stop him—but she didn't. The kiss deepened. Her hands clamped onto the soft material of his shirt, and she let them run down the length of his arms.

She wanted to feel his weight on her, pressing her

into the flowers. She heard herself moan as he traced her lips with his tongue. It had been so long…so long.

And it felt so good.

"Beth?"

She heard her name, a mere whisper on the wind, like the butterfly that had danced on the white flower.

"Beth." His voice was strained. "I'd really like to finish what we started here, but I have to get back."

Her eyes shot open. Her cheeks flushed warm. "Oh!" What was she thinking? What was she doing? "I—I don't know what came over me." She scrambled to get up, to move as far away from Jake as she could. "I'm sorry. I must have…"

"No. Don't apologize! I've wanted to do that since you got off the plane."

She wanted to take the next plane back. "You must think I'm just another one of Jake Dixon's groupies, right?"

"I never said that."

"But that's the way I feel."

"We both just did what we wanted to. What's the harm?"

The harm was that she wanted more from him than just one kiss. A lot more.

She brushed herself off. "Let's just get back to the others." She picked up the saddle and lugged it over to where Thunder was grazing. She saddled the horse and pulled the cinch as hard as she could.

Glancing back, she saw that Jake hadn't moved. He was sitting, propped up by his arms, chewing on a blade of grass and watching her.

"You have to knee him in the tummy," Jake said.

"I can't."

"Then the same thing will happen again."

"Will you do it?"

"Yeah, but I'm going to need a hand up. Will you get me the rope hanging from Lance's saddle?"

"I'll help you up."

"I'm too heavy for you."

She did what he asked. "Are we going to drag you behind Lance all the way back to the Gold Buckle?"

He laughed. "You'd like that, wouldn't you."

She raised her eyebrows. "Well…"

She watched as he worked the rope. He had it moving in a circle over his head. With a sharp jerk of his arm, he lassoed Lance's saddle horn. She had to admire his skill.

"Will you lead Lance slowly? Too fast and I'm going to go headfirst—and you'll get your wish."

She led Lance as slowly as she could until Jake was on his feet and had dropped the rope. After a while, when he was steady, he walked over to Thunder and put a knee in the horse's side. Beth groaned.

"What kind of gentleman are you?" Jake asked. "You shouldn't have done that to the lady." Turning back to her, he held out his hand, and she thought he was going to kiss her again. She took his hand, but instead of another breathtaking kiss, he handed her Thunder's reins. "He's all set. You can get back on now."

In one smooth motion, he was on Lance's back and gathering up the rope and looping it in a circle. Tying the rope to the saddle, he squinted at the distance.

"If you're ready, we could gallop across the meadow and catch up to the others. How about it?"

She felt a warm rush of excitement. “Let’s go.” It only took her three tries to get into the saddle this time.

He gave her some instruction. “Just relax. Feel his gait and go with it. Feel the motion. If you want to slow down, pull very gently on the reins. If things get out of control, yell and I’ll stop him. Ready?”

She nodded.

“Let’s go!” he said.

Thunder was definitely up for a run. It felt as if the horse had launched himself off a springboard. The meadow was a blur of color as she raced behind Jake. The wind licked at her hat, so in a quick motion she pushed it down tighter on her head.

Jake set the pace. At first she thought it was much too fast, but as she got more confident, she wanted to go even faster.

She decided it would be fun to try to pass him, so she nudged Thunder a little with her heels. She leaned forward like jockeys do at a race. The horse’s muscles moved beneath her thighs. His mane flew in her face. The wind whipped her cheeks. She could hear Thunder’s blowing as he ran, hear the thud of the horses’ hooves.

“Whooo-eee!” Jake yelled. He seemed to be enjoying the race as much as she.

Still she didn’t have a prayer in beating him. The big black was too fast for Thunder, and Jake was too good a horseman for her.

Beth could see other riders up ahead as Jake slowed Lance to a walk and Thunder followed suit.

“Now *that* was fun!” she said.

“Terrific! You did a great job. We’ll have to do that again sometime.”

"I'd love to, but next time, I want a little head start."

He grinned but shook his head. "No way."

They rejoined the others and slowed to a meandering walk. Finally, she was able to reflect on the kiss they'd shared. She touched her lips. Had they really kissed? The butterflies still in her stomach told her they had. Passionately. Hard.

But she reminded herself that nothing more could come of it. They were from two different worlds. And besides, she didn't want to get involved with anyone, especially not Jake Dixon. He was the type of man she could easily lose her heart to. And she didn't want a man in her life, not now. She was happy living with her son, just the two of them.

But first and foremost, Jake Dixon was a drinker. She remembered the altercation at the airport, and then seeing him drinking last night. No way was she going to let another drinker in her life.

More than that, he had hurt someone when drinking, and she couldn't risk that ever again. She had ignored it once and Kevin had paid the price.

Then why had she accepted his invitation to go out tonight?

The first thing Beth noticed when her eyes adjusted to the dim light and smoke of the Last Chance Saloon was that people were sitting on saddles at the bar. Saddles for bar stools were a bit unusual, but that wasn't what bothered her.

"I thought you were taking me dancing. This place is a bar."

"It has a bar, but it's also a pool hall, a meeting place

and a restaurant. It's where singers get some audience time with their bands. It's where we can dance. We don't have to sit at the bar."

He guided her to a small table by the dance floor, which was packed with people doing some kind of line dance.

Jake's foot tapped to the music. "Ready to boot scoot?"

She tried to forget that she hated bars. "I should have told you to wear steel-toed boots," she joked.

"Never fear. Just follow me." He held out his hands and she took them.

With both his hands on her waist, they did some quick fox-trot-like steps. He was easy to follow. Then the tempo of the music increased and he had her twirling and promenading.

"Ouch!" Jake said, as she stepped on his foot.

"Sorry, this is all new to me."

"Yee-ow!"

She laughed. "What are your feet doing under mine, anyway?" She was having a great time, and knew he was teasing her, but soon she realized that Jake was favoring his leg. "I'm kind of hot," she lied. "Would you mind if we sat down for a while?"

"No problem." He led her off the dance floor and pulled out a chair for her, then just about collapsed onto his. He stretched his right leg out in front of him and let out a long breath.

"How about something to drink?" he asked, when the waitress came to their table.

"A glass of ice water, please."

"A glass of ice water for the lady, and I'll have a beer."

She cringed at the thought of watching him drink. She realized that not everyone had a problem as extensive as Brad's, but she hated what alcohol did to people. The waitress returned and set the water in front of her and beer before Jake. Before Beth could blink, he raised the bottle up to her in a toast and took a long draw. Setting it down, he licked his lips as though he didn't want to waste a drop.

She didn't want to see Jake drink, didn't want to watch him start down that path. She excused herself, went into the ladies room, splashed water on her face and fixed her makeup. Taking a couple of deep breaths, she walked back to the table—to find Jake surrounded by several gorgeous women.

He stood when he saw her approach. "Ladies, would you excuse me? Beth and I are going to dance."

Jake's "groupies" parted after eyeballing her from head to toe. They reluctantly waved goodbye to him. Two gave suggestive winks, and one heavily made-up, maroon-haired, well-endowed young woman slipped a piece of paper—with her phone number?—into the pocket of his shirt.

He held out his hand to Beth. She took it.

"Feeling better?" he asked.

"Yes." *No,* she thought as she spied his empty beer bottle.

"Good. Let's dance."

It was a waltz, so it seemed natural for Jake to hold her tight against his strong body. The smoky, sensual voice of the lead singer and the musky scent of Jake's Bull-istic made her remember that she'd be alone in the Trail Boss Cabin tonight.

She sighed, feeling more relaxed as they swayed to Chris LeDoux's song about the Powder River and the prairie sky, moonlit evenings and dancing under the stars.

Her hand moved on the back of his neck and her fingers itched to touch the soft, feathery hair showing beneath his hat, so she did. He moaned slightly and flashed her a grin.

His blue eyes twinkled in amusement. "You're not teasing me like you did in the meadow, are you?"

"Teasing you? I don't tease." She just wanted to touch his hair.

"What do you call it, then? Flirting?"

"I don't know how to flirt, Jake."

"Then be careful. When a woman's interested in me, I want a clear message."

Truth was, she didn't know what she was doing. One second, she was telling herself she was going to keep her distance. The next, she was running her fingers through his hair.

In the meadow, she had just wanted a kiss. That's all. A simple kiss. It had backfired, and now she was dreaming of Jake in her cabin. In her bed.

She'd buried her own needs, emotions and feelings long ago to concentrate on Kevin. Now she didn't know what to do with her own. They were bubbling to the surface and overflowing. How could she contain them?

Jake stepped back a bit, took her wrist and pressed her hand over his heart. He held it there and she could feel his heart beating, strong and true. He settled the bottom of his cheek on her temple. They swayed to the music.

"Mmm...nice," he said.

"Seems like you're sending *me* a clear message."

"That I am, darlin'. That I am."

"Be careful or I'll step on your feet."

He chuckled and pulled her closer. "I'll take that chance."

She could feel his heat through her blouse, feel the warmth of his breath on her neck, the scratch of his denim on hers.

Beth realized that they were indeed flirting, engaged in some kind of ritual that might lead to more. While that thrilled her, it also scared her to death.

Beth liked being held in Jake's arms. She didn't want the song to end, didn't want the moment to end. But it did.

They parted, and he led her back to the table.

Their order was there. Another glass of water. Another beer.

She took a sip of water. He took a couple chugs of beer.

Reality.

Beth looked at the band. She couldn't look at Jake drinking.

He had started to be her hero, the way he was Kevin's hero. He was a good man. He was great with kids. He had a good heart. He was respected by all the cowboys, his peers.

Darn it. She might as well admit that she was interested in him. But could she get past his drinking?

Two young women in tight blouses and jeans came over to the table to have Jake autograph cocktail napkins. They carried long-necked bottles of beer and plopped two down before Jake.

"For the best bull rider in the business," the redhead gushed.

"Thank you," Jake said, looking amused.

A blonde with hair down to her waist, a skimpy black tank top and jeans that looked painted on, appeared and set down yet another beer for Jake. She lifted her shirt for Jake to autograph her bare midriff.

"Write 'To Trixie. It was a great night last night. With love, Jake Dixon,'" she instructed.

He laughed. "I'll leave that part out until I know for a fact it's true."

She tossed her hair back and pursed her candy-apple-red lips. "Anytime, anywhere, Jake."

He hesitated and glanced at Beth. "Trixie, if you don't mind, how about if I just autograph a cocktail napkin for you."

Beth appreciated his consideration. "Oh, go for the stomach, Jake." She grinned. "It's much more interesting than a cocktail napkin."

"Nope. I make it a practice not to autograph body parts." He wrote his name on a napkin and handed it to the woman.

Trixie bent over, giving him a nice view of her cleavage, and wrote her name and number on another napkin. She tucked it into the front pocket of his shirt. He was going to need another pocket if the cocktail napkins kept accumulating.

Trixie shot a triumphant look at Beth, tossed her hair and sauntered away.

Jake now had three new bottles of beer in front of him, one in his hand, and a grin as wide as the Wyoming sky.

Just like Brad.

She'd had enough. She needed to get far away from the Last Chance Saloon, far away from drunken laughter, buckle bunnies, and Jake Dixon's rising stockpile of beer bottles.

Beth grabbed her pocketbook and stood. "I'm going back to the ranch."

Chapter Seven

Jake had thought that Beth was having a good time.

But now her eyes squinted at him. Her lips were locked together in a thin line. She was madder than a bull in the bucking chutes with a rider on his back.

If he lived to be a hundred, he'd never understand women. He took off his hat and raked his fingers through his hair. Then it hit him. He knew what was wrong.

"Those ladies meant nothing to me. You don't have to be jealous."

"Jealous? Me?" She stood with her hands on her hips. "Of all the conceited, thick-headed, addle-brained—"

"Whoa!" He held up his hand. "I get the message. But if you're not jealous, what is it?"

"Beer." She spit out the word as if it left a bad taste in her mouth.

"Beer?"

"Is there an echo here? Yes, beer!"

He moved his hat back. "What about it?"

"You're drinking it."

"So?" He thought for a while, then slapped his head with the palm of his hand. "Oh...Beth, I'm sorry. If my drinking a beer bothered you, why didn't you tell me?"

"I've been telling you since I met you. I haven't made any bones about how much I hate drinking."

"You have. You're right. I'm sorry, but I wasn't going to have more than one. I'm driving, you know," he said. "I'm not that much of an idiot."

"You had three beers in front of you," she reminded him.

"I know, but that doesn't mean I'm going to drink them all."

"Oh?"

"I wasn't."

She stared a hole right through him, weighing and measuring the truth of his statement. "Well...okay. Maybe I overreacted."

"Maybe you did." He offered her a hand, and she sat back down. "I'd like to dance with you some more."

When she hesitated, he pulled a set of keys out of his pocket and passed them to her. "Maybe this'll make you feel better. You have my word—only one beer."

She put the keys in her purse. "Thank you, Jake," she said quietly. "It's just that I get so crazy."

"No problem. I should have remembered. I apologize."

Shyly she offered him her hand, and he reached for it across the table. Jake motioned to the waitress to clear the bottles away.

"Give 'em away, Connie," he said to the waitress. "They're still cold."

Connie gave him a strange look but cleared the table.

"And bring us two ice waters, please," Jake said.

The waitress raised an eyebrow but didn't say a word.

"Thanks," Beth said, when Connie walked away.

"No problem. Now, how about a little two-steppin'?"

"Sure."

Jake lucked out. Big John McCoy had a microphone and was gathering everyone up for two-step lessons. Jake didn't have to do much, other than stand next to Beth and follow along. After a while, he motioned to his leg, told her to stay and dance, and he went back to the table to sit for a while. He could have stuck it out, but he enjoyed watching her more.

As she concentrated on doing the steps, her grin was as big as the Wyoming sky. Every time she missed a step or banged into someone, she laughed or apologized and looked like she was having the time of her life. Good. She needed some fun.

He tipped his chair back, put his feet up on a vacant seat and crossed his ankles. He had to admit that he hadn't wanted to go on this date, but it was turning out okay. Except for his Big Beer Mistake. Beth was good company when she forgot to obsess over Kevin...and drinking.

He liked her enough, but she had a wheelbarrow full of problems to sort through and he wasn't going to get involved with her. As she had told him herself, he was no psychiatrist. Besides, Kevin had volunteered the information that Beth hadn't gone out with a man since his father died.

He could tell that by the kiss they'd shared.

What the hell had made him kiss her in the meadow? It had rocked him down to the heels of his boots.

He wouldn't mind getting up close and personal with her for a week, but in the long run, it wouldn't work. She had to know that from the start.

She had a permanent residence. She went to parent-teacher meetings. She had an office job.

He was bulls and blood, food in a bag from a drive-through window, cheap hotels, thousands of frequent-flier miles and even more thousands in medical bills.

He'd only hurt her, and she'd been hurt enough.

They had nothing in common except one week at the Gold Buckle Ranch.

Maybe that would be enough.

More beers appeared at his table. He smiled his thanks, signed autographs, stretched out his legs and kept calling for Connie to pass them around.

Big John McCoy paired Beth with a tall, lean cowboy that Jake recognized as a bronc rider from around Kaycee. The cowboy slipped his arm around Beth and pulled her much too close to him, as far as Jake was concerned.

While Beth was two-stepping like a Texas native, he wondered if his leg was ever going to get better. He'd settle for it not constantly hurting him. As he grew older, it took him longer to react and to get away from a bull set on killing him. It might be only a second or two more, but that meant the difference between a minor injury and one that was debilitating—or fatal.

Yet he loved it—the adrenaline rush, the cheers of the crowd, the sponsors, the TV appearances, the fans—oh, the fans. He loved the fans. He loved all of it.

Beth came back to a table with more beer bottles on it than when she'd left. She frowned slightly.

"Now, don't worry. I'm giving them all away," he said. "Just as soon as Connie comes this way again."

As soon as Beth sat down, a camera flash went off in his eyes, followed by another.

"Well, there he is! Mr. King of the Bull Riders. And look at all those bottles of beer! Another great picture for my newspaper."

Jake knew the voice. "Harvey Trumble. Not again. Who hates me that much that they had to call you and tell you I was here?"

Beth turned toward the man. "Mr. Trumble, Jake is not drinking. Those are not his beer bottles. People have been buying them for him. So if you write otherwise in your paper, it would be untrue."

"Pardon me, miss, but this doesn't concern you." Harvey's words were abrupt and sarcastic.

With difficulty, Jake stood. "Yes, it does concern her. You're interrupting our dance lesson." It seemed that half the place stood and moved toward Jake's table in case he needed help.

With one glance, Harvey knew he was outnumbered.

"Harvey, I'm going to tell you one last time. Keith tripped and fell and broke his arm during a brawl here," Jake said. "He was making unwelcome advances toward my sister. I tried to reason with him, and he threw a punch. It turned into a free-for-all with everyone getting involved. He fell. End of story."

"You said that my son wasn't good enough for your sister."

"I remember."

"And you were drinking."

Jake nodded. "That's right, but I'm not tonight, so quit bothering me, Harvey. If Keith wants to talk to me about the whole thing, I'd be glad to sit down with him."

Harvey pointed a finger at Jake's chest. "This isn't over yet."

"As far as I'm concerned, it is."

Harvey broke into a slow, sly grin. "Hey, I have a proposition for you, Dixon."

"What's that?"

"The night of your big rodeo—"

Jake hooked his thumbs into his belt loops. "It's not a rodeo. It's bull riding."

"Whatever," he said through clamped teeth. "If you ride Twister, I'll donate some money to Wheelchair Rodeo on behalf of my paper and lay off you."

"Who?" Beth asked.

"Twister's a bounty bull. No one has ever made eight seconds on him," Jake explained. "Thirty guys have tried him but they were all bucked off. His owner has increased the pot by increments of five thousand, so now it's up to a hundred and fifty thousand bucks."

Jake turned to Harvey to find himself in a cloud of cigar smoke. He held his breath, waved the smoke away and stepped back. "I'll get the hundred and fifty thousand from the stock contractor who owns Twister, Harvey. What are you going to donate to Wheelchair Rodeo?"

"A half-million over the course of three years."

Jake put on a poker face. That was more than he had ever expected. That kind of money would help—immensely. Knowing how to play to the crowd, he bluffed. "Aw, c'mon, Harvey, for such a good cause and all tax deductible, I think your paper could afford a million over the course of three years."

Harvey's mouth opened and closed like that of a fish, as the crowd cheered their encouragement.

"What do you have to worry about? Your money is safe. You said so yourself that I'm a has-been bull rider. I don't have a prayer of riding Twister."

"It's a deal." Sputtering and stammering, Harvey stormed out of the bar.

Jake couldn't believe Harvey had taken the bait.

When he was able to concentrate again on Beth, he saw her confusion. "Sorry. I'll bet that this is the worst date you've ever been on."

"It's the *only* date I've been on in the past ten years." She shrugged. "But this is exactly how I remember them."

Damn, she could make him laugh.

"Let's dance," he said. Dancing was safe. He held out his hand. When his fingers closed around hers, he felt…protective. He wanted to cushion her from any more heartache, any more pain.

But Beth Conroy was tough. She wouldn't accept his protection.

He took her in his arms. It was a slow song and the lead singer was trying to imitate the gravelly voice of Willie Nelson. It was perfect shuffling and swaying music.

"Jake?"

"Yeah?"

"Can you ride Twister?"

"I don't know. He's bucked off a lot of good guys. I'm sure as hell going to try my best. A million bucks will go far in Wheelchair Rodeo."

"But you're injured. I see you limping and trying to straighten your back, and—"

"Bull riding's a tough sport. We don't have multimillion-dollar contracts like the basketball, football and baseball players have. A lot of cowboys ride injured all the time. It's their job. They have families to support. Only a few who are really, really lucky and really good can earn a lot of money—most of which comes from endorsements and sponsors. Until recently, I've been one of those few."

"As Kevin says, 'Jake Dixon's the best.'" She laid her head on his shoulder.

Moments later he heard Beth singing to the music. He liked that. "A country music fan?"

She looked up, her green eyes sparkling in the dim light. "I listen to it all the time."

When the song ended he didn't want to let her go, but they had to part when Big John McCoy put a meaty hand on Jake's shoulder and turned him toward the crowd sitting at the tables.

Beth tried to back away, but Jake held on to her hand.

Big John spoke into a microphone. "Ladies and gentlemen, I'm sure you know one of the best bull riders in the business, our own Jake Dixon."

Jake waved to the audience and tipped his hat to the cheers.

"Jake, you've been injured a lot, and there's a lot of talk that your career is over. What do you have to say to that?"

Beth squeezed his hand. He looked at her and she nodded at him with confidence. It warmed him clear down to his boots.

"Well, Big John, we have a saying in bull riding. It's not *if* you're going to get injured, it's *when* and *how bad.* I got injured pretty bad in Loughlin, but I've been down before."

Big John nodded. "What would you respond to those who say that your career is over?"

"I'd tell them that I'm coming back and I'm going to be better than ever."

"Thank you, Jake Dixon!" Big John waited until the applause died down. "Anything else you'd like to say to your friends here?"

Jake didn't hesitate. "Many of you know that Wheelchair Rodeo is in progress right now at the Gold Buckle Ranch, and everyone has been generous in their support. I'd like to thank everyone, on behalf of the kids."

Big John took off his cowboy hat and spoke. "I think we should pass the hat for the kids—right, everyone?"

There was another round of applause.

"Thank you," Jake said. "And I'd like to remind everyone that the Jake Dixon Gold Buckle Challenge will be Saturday night at the Mountain Springs Arena, so come on over. Proceeds will be donated to Wheelchair Rodeo. And I just found out that Harvey Trumble, the owner of the *Wyoming Journal,* is going to be sponsoring me on the bounty bull. If I ride him, he's donating a hefty chunk of money to Wheelchair Rodeo."

Jake waited for the applause and hooting to end. "It'll be a good time as usual. So come and support this good cause and maybe get on TV." He tapped his hat brim once more. "Thanks, everyone. Now, let's dance!"

The band kicked up a two-step and he swung Beth into position. "Let's see what you've learned, or how rusty I am."

"But your leg—"

"I'll stop when I need to."

Beth Conroy was a quick study, and Jake tried to make it to the end of the song, but the band was carrying on with chorus after chorus. He finally knew he had to sit down.

"My boots are still like new and I don't have any broken toes. You can go back to Arizona and show them how you can do the Texas two-step, Wyoming-style."

She smiled. "I'll do that."

He guided her back to their table. They both reached for their glasses of ice water and took a long draw.

"Drinking water isn't so bad, is it?" she asked, clinking her glass against his.

He really wanted a beer. "It'll do."

She ran her finger down the dewy glass. "I can't help but notice that you're in a lot of pain. If you are bucked off, will you be able to get up fast enough to get away from the bull?"

He leaned over the table. They were mere inches apart. "Darlin', if I didn't know better, I'd think you cared about me."

He could see her struggling to find the right words. "I-I...don't like to see anyone hurt. What does your doctor say?"

He hesitated. "He said I should take more time off." He rocked his chair back on its two rear legs and looked around. Wasn't anyone going to rescue him from this conversation? No midriffs to sign? No autographs needed on cocktail napkins?

"Then why don't you do what the doctor says?"

"If I can ride the bounty bull, Wheelchair Rodeo will be set for a long time."

"And if you can't?"

"Wheelchair Rodeo will continue to rely on contributions, and I'm going to ride in the Challenge because it's my event," he said simply.

"Why?"

"I'm the organizer. My name's on it. It's called the Jake Dixon Gold Buckle Challenge for a reason. I'm going to ride. I *need* to ride. I ride bulls. That's what I do."

"Oh, for heaven's sake! Do you want to end up in a wheelchair?" she shouted over the band. Her eyes widened with shock and she clamped her lips together.

He pushed his hat back with his thumb. That was just the question his doctor had asked him.

"I'm sorry," Beth said. "It's none of my business."

"That's right."

"Just like when you say I'm overprotective of Kevin, it's none of your business."

"Right again."

She gathered up her purse. "Shall we go now?"

He'd upset her again. Wasn't this the perfect ending to one hell of a strange night?

She was quiet on the ride home. At one point she fell asleep, so he put his arm around her shoulder and tried to pull her closer to him, but he woke her instead.

She grunted. "What?"

"Lay your head on my shoulder if you want to sleep, so you don't bang it against the window."

She rubbed her eyes and sat up straighter. "I'm fine."

"Suit yourself."

Ah, yes. The Jake Dixon charm. He'd been goaded into taking Beth out. Then he couldn't drink, couldn't dance and couldn't fight.

What kind of cowboy was he?

Jake walked Beth to the door of the Trail Boss Cabin. He couldn't remember when he'd been such a bonehead on a date. First, there was the Great Beer Mistake, then the Harvey Trumble Fiasco. Finally, he tells her to butt out of his life.

He was so tired, his eyes were burning from the smoke at the Last Chance and he could barely stand. But he wanted to set things right with her.

Yet at her cabin door, he was at a loss for words.

"It was a great night. Thanks," he managed to mumble. He didn't understand it. He'd been interviewed by all the sports biggies, but he couldn't connect two worthwhile sentences in front of Beth Conroy right now.

But he couldn't stand the sadness in her eyes. He'd been too hard on her during the butt-out conversation.

So he did what he'd wanted to do all night. He pulled her to him and kissed her.

Her arms went around his neck, and he took it as a sign that she wanted more. He deepened the kiss. His hands itched to touch her, to discover her body, to feel her warmth. He inhaled her scent, which was like musky roses.

She broke away, took a deep breath. He could feel her wrists pulse where he held her. She was as affected by their kiss as he. "Good night, Jake. Thanks for the evening out." Beth hesitated for a moment. "I'd ask you in, but tomorrow is a big day. We both need to get some sleep."

He knew a brush-off when he heard one.

"Good night, Beth. See you in the morning."

He watched as she closed the door, then he hobbled back to the ranch house.

They just didn't mesh. She could be fun, and they'd had a few laughs, but when they crossed some invisible border, one of them got their hackles up.

He should just keep his distance.

Beth took a quick, hot shower to get the odor of cigarette smoke out of her hair. She was exhausted, but instead of sleeping, she thought about Jake Dixon.

It had been an unusual night, but there were a few things that had made a considerable impression on her. Jake had refrained from drinking because of her, and he'd handled Harvey Trumble with much more patience than she would have.

One thing she never thought about much was Jake's popularity—his celebrity, or whatever it was called. She remembered the group gathered around him at the airport, and the crowd that had supported him at the Last Chance Saloon. She remembered the woman, Trixie, who'd asked him to autograph her stomach, and how he didn't want to embarrass Beth by doing it. Interesting.

They lived such different lives. He was country; she was city. He was fairly rich; she rented apartments. He could have any woman he wanted; she was a widow coping with a lot of guilt and a son in a wheelchair....

Kevin!

She shot upright in bed. She hadn't thought of Kevin in hours. What kind of a mother was she?

She took a deep, calming breath and made herself relax. Kevin was fine. He was having fun. And so was she. There was nothing to worry about.

But after years of conditioning, how could she stop?

The next morning, after a fitful sleep, Beth shrugged into a sweatshirt and hurried out the door for the flag-raising ceremony. It was a foggy morning, but the sun would soon burn the fog away. It was going to be another lovely day at the Gold Buckle Ranch.

By the time the Pledge of Allegiance, Dex's prayer and the day's announcements were over, the fog was gone.

She scanned the crowd of kids for Kevin. He spotted her, grinned and waved. That little gesture made her decide that he was doing okay and wasn't missing her. He turned, and she followed the direction of his gaze. His smile went even wider and his wave stronger. Jake Dixon was walking toward him.

They exchanged manly handshakes. Jake ruffled his hair, and Kevin didn't seem to mind it in the least. The two of them clicked. No matter what, she was glad that Kevin had had the opportunity to meet Jake and get to know him.

And deep down, she was glad that she had had the same opportunity.

"Is everyone having a great time?" Dex Dixon shouted.

"Yeah!"

The cowboys tossed their hats in the air. Beth loved how they got the kids excited. Their deep voices mixed with the high-pitched cheers of the kids echoed across the grounds of the ranch.

"Today, we're going to get ready for the big trail ride tomorrow. There'll be more riding and roping practice and we're going to hear about how the pioneers settled the West. There's some other things planned, too, but first—" Dex pointed to several hay wagons coming down the lane "—first, we are going to take a hayride to breakfast. Cookie's fixing up something special by the river."

The kids squealed.

"Everyone go with your volunteer and they'll take you to your assigned wagon. Of course, our other guests are welcome to join us. There's plenty of room and plenty of food."

The cowboys and the volunteers began wheeling the kids away. Ramps were in place. Soon the wagons were loaded. Kevin was one of the first to get on.

"Mom! Mom! Aren't you coming?" Kevin yelled.

"I think I'll stay here today, sweetie."

"C'mon, Mom!"

Jake appeared at her side. "What's stopping you?"

"I was giving Kevin some distance."

Jake raised an eyebrow. "If I didn't know any better, I'd think that you're taking some of my unwanted advice."

"Maybe."

"Good, but forget it this time." He took her arm. "Kevin wants you to go."

Standing so close to him reminded her of the kiss

they had shared last night. A kiss that had curled her toes and kept her up tossing and turning and thinking of him.

"Scrambled eggs, country sausage, home fries and Cookie's special biscuits on a blanket alongside the Silver River. Later, Clint Scully's going to spin a story or two for the kids. What more could you ask for?" Jake asked.

"Less grease." Beth laughed.

He laughed. "Never. Cookie wouldn't know how to cook without grease."

"So I've discovered."

"What do you say?"

"It sounds wonderful."

He motioned with his hand. "Let's go, then."

She walked with him to the wagon, where Kevin was already in position. Jake helped her up the ramp. She sat on a bale of hay beside Kevin, and Jake sat next to her.

"Are you having a good time?" Beth asked her son.

"Awesome! It's just so cool here, Mom. I wish we could stay forever."

"I have a job. You have school. When our vacation is over, we have to go home. You know that."

"But you can get a job here, and I can go to school here. I can have my own horse and…and…"

"Kevin…" *Let me worry about the future,* she thought. She was good at it, since she worried about it nearly every day of their lives.

"Hey, Kev, how's your roping coming?" Jake asked, and she was glad for the change of conversation. "I think you're a real contender for the Gold Buckle."

"Really, Jake?"

"Really." Jake nodded. "I think your competition is Haley Jo and maybe Alex, but I think you can win it with a little more practice." He winked at Beth. "Besides, you have the *official* Jake Dixon rope."

Beth winked back. "Well, that decides it. Haley Jo and Alex don't have a chance."

Clint Scully pulled out a guitar and started singing "Home on the Range," which seemed to be his anthem. Everyone joined in. More songs followed, along with good-natured joking among the cowboys and kids.

Beth laughed loudly and frequently, sang at the top of her lungs and clapped along with the kids. It was a beautiful day, made even better by Kevin and Jake's company.

When they arrived at the river, Kevin wheeled away to listen to Clint Scully's story.

Beth smiled at the cowboy next to her. "Jake, I'd like to thank you for changing the subject back there. Kevin gets so carried away."

He looked out at the distant mountains. "I can't blame the boy. It's beautiful out here."

"It's beautiful in Lizard Rock, too."

"In an apartment building?"

"Well, no, but we can drive to one of the local parks." Actually, lately she hadn't had the time to take Kevin anywhere except to doctors' visits and to the hospital for tests.

"It's not the same as all this, is it?"

"Not for a little boy with rodeo and horses and bulls on his mind, but it's the best I can do. Sometimes I feel like it's just not enough, no matter what." She sighed, then blurted, "And Kevin should be walking, but he's not. I have to take him to Boston."

It shocked her that she had just divulged her big worry to Jake Dixon without a moment's hesitation.

"I'm sorry," she said. "I'm babbling and whining and I can't stand myself about now. Maybe you should just go join the others while I walk this mood off."

"You can tell me what's on your mind. Of course you're worried about Kevin not walking."

He took her arm, steadying her as she stumbled on uneven ground. They continued walking.

"You know, there's something about this place that's making me crazy. I never tell anyone my business or my worries. What is it about you?"

"Maybe I'm a good listener."

"Maybe I have too much time to think here. Back home, I never have this kind of time."

"Let me get this straight—you don't like having too much time to think?"

"Correct."

Jake picked up a small stone and skimmed it across the river. "It's bad to think?"

"It is for me. I start to obsess."

"Just keep in mind that usually you can come to some kind of resolution when you have time to think about a problem. Then you can start to work on a plan. But obsessing doesn't do any good."

"Do you get a lot of problems solved here, Jake?"

"Usually, but lately I haven't had time to think."

She laughed. "You have time now."

"Okay. I think that I'm starving and need some coffee. So let's go and visit Cookie." Jake motioned for her to come with him. "There. Now, wasn't that easy?"

"That was a cop-out, Jake Dixon."

Chapter Eight

Jake took a seat in the picnic pavilion and stretched out his right leg. He enjoyed the sounds of laughter, good-natured teasing and shouting that drifted on the breeze. That's what he liked to hear at the Gold Buckle Ranch, the sound of children being children and having a good time.

He was the most content when the campers arrived at the ranch. All his work throughout the year, along with the help of his mother and father who believed in Wheelchair Rodeo as much as he did, paid off whenever he looked at their happy faces.

"How's the leg, Jake?"

Shoot. He'd been hoping not to run into Trot, known officially as Dr. Michael Trotter at Casper General Hospital.

"It's doing better," he lied.

"Doesn't seem much better the way you're favoring it. I want to check it and check your back. Stop in at the infirmary and let me take a touch and feel. I also want updated X rays. You can go to Casper Gen and get them done."

"Sorry, Doc. No time."

Trot took a gulp of coffee and raised a dark eyebrow. "*Make* time. I'll bet my diplomas that your fracture isn't healing right and your back is… Hell, we'll cross that bridge later."

Jake opened his mouth to say something, but the doctor held up a hand. "Dammit, Jake. You're not invincible."

"I'm doing okay."

"Doesn't look it, and it's only going to get worse if you don't let me operate on you."

"Are you nagging me, Trot?"

"Whatever it takes. Are you still planning on riding in the Challenge?"

"You know I am. Plus I'm riding a bounty bull before that."

"You'd better buy a wheelchair of your own, then. I'm advising against it." Trot drained his coffee. "Out of curiosity, who's the bounty bull?"

"Twister."

"Great." Trot raised his eyes to the sky. "While you're at Casper Gen, we'll have your head examined, too."

Beth took a sip of coffee to wash down the fried potatoes that had caught in her throat. She hadn't meant to listen in, but they were sitting right behind her.

She knew how much riding the bounty bull and riding in his own event meant to Jake, but heavens, he certainly didn't want to end up in a wheelchair himself. Beth didn't know if the doctor was talking about a permanent injury or a temporary condition if he rode. But either way, why would Jake want to take that chance?

Because it meant a million dollars to Wheelchair Rodeo.

And the Challenge had his name on it.

Those were pretty important reasons to Jake. Important enough for him to put his health and his life on the line.

It was none of her concern. Whatever Jake Dixon did was his business, not hers. He'd already told her as much.

Beth helped some of the kids get their breakfast. Special picnic tables had been made so they could wheel their chairs right up to the table. No doubt it was Jake's idea, and he and his friends had probably done the work. If he could make a drawing for her with the measurements, she could get one made for Kevin back in Lizard Rock and put it outside on her small patio.

A dull ache settled in her chest. Kevin should be walking, but since he wasn't, she really needed to take him to Boston so another specialist could evaluate him and figure out what was wrong. She'd do that the minute she got home.

Home.

She had to admit that she wouldn't mind moving to Wyoming, but what she could afford in Wyoming was pretty much what she could afford in Arizona. Nothing much. So far, the only business-type places she'd seen in Mountain Springs where she could get a job were the Last Chance Saloon and the gas station next to it. She'd love a job at the Gold Buckle Ranch, but from what she could tell, it was entirely run by volunteers.

She'd have to get a job in a nearby city like Casper. That would defeat the purpose of Kevin moving here.

He also wanted a horse, and she'd love to give him one. She didn't know the first thing about horses, other than that she could saddle one—well, kind of. A horse was a major expense. So was the care and feeding of one.

While the kids ate and talked, Beth noticed they all had much more color in their cheeks than when they'd arrived. They were more animated, and they'd made new friends. It was good for them to get outside more, socialize with kids in the same situation, forget that they had problems—and be cowboys for a while.

She was glad that Kevin was participating in Wheelchair Rodeo. So far everything was going well. Any earlier fears about Jake's drinking had been banished to the back of her mind, but she was still going to be vigilant.

Emily Dixon called for the kids to make a circle around the campfire. Clint Scully was waiting for them. He announced that he was going to tell a story about "some pioneers who got stuck in a snowstorm in this very valley, back in 'bout 1880."

I hope it's not the Donner party, Beth thought.

"You're not thinking again, are you?" Jake asked as he joined her at the picnic table.

"Yes and no. I'm listening to Clint, thinking about how much the kids are enjoying everything. You have a fabulous program. As the mother of a son who's just thrilled to be here, I want to thank you from the bottom of my heart."

He shrugged. "No one loves Wheelchair Rodeo more than I do, except maybe my folks. The cowboys love it too. For some, it's the family they don't have. They love the kids, and more than one tough cowboy gets a little water in his eyes on occasion." He nodded toward the circle. "Those kids are the ones who are really tough. I couldn't sit in a wheelchair the rest of my life."

"If you had a choice, why would you?"

Jake looked down at the cup of coffee in his hands. He seemed a million miles away.

She left him to his thoughts for a while, then said, "You're not thinking again, are you?"

He looked up, chuckled, and returned to staring into his coffee.

She nudged his arm. "Even tough cowboys need to talk." She hesitated, then jumped right in. "I couldn't help but hear what the doctor said to you."

He nodded.

"I'll go with you to Casper if you'd like some company."

He looked up and pushed his hat back with a thumb in that characteristic gesture that she'd forever associate with Jake. "That's not necessary, since I won't be going. I can't spare the time."

"I'm sure there's nothing on the schedule today that someone else can't handle. Besides, I'll never come back here, and I'd love to see more of your beautiful state."

He scratched his forehead. "You want to blow a whole day in Casper keeping me company? Why the hell would you want to do that?"

"Because your company's not all that bad. Because of all you've done for Kevin and the other kids. Because you found a horse with four white socks and taught me how to ride. But mostly because I don't want to see you end up in a wheelchair, either temporarily or permanently."

"Sounds like you care."

"Of course I care," she snapped, then lowered her voice. She didn't want him to mistake her concern for interest, so she added, "I'd care about anyone in your situation."

"Oh," he said, raising an eyebrow, seeming disappointed.

"Say you'll do it, Jake. Go tell Dr. Trotter to make the arrangements," she insisted.

"I'm going to ride in the Challenge even if they tell me I can't."

"Then let's go find out how disabled you're going to be after you do so." The sarcasm didn't become her, but maybe it would work on him. "So what do you say? They're only a few pictures. Think of it as your fan club wanting photos for your Web site."

He chuckled, drained his coffee, thought a while. "I'll see if my folks can handle things. If so, then I'll have Trot make the call. You go tell Kevin. I'll borrow a couple of horses, and we can ride back to the ranch and hop in my pickup."

"Okay."

Beth watched as Jake walked away, his limp even more pronounced on the uneven terrain. She was amazed that he was doing what the doctor had suggested. And she was going with him. Why? Why did she care so much about this man? Jake had asked her the same question, and at first she had answered him truthfully. But deep inside, she knew there was more.

She cared for him. She admired him. She loved how he handled the kids, especially Kevin, and how they adored him in return. He was a good man.

Looking around, she saw Emily Dixon walking toward her, smiling. "How can I thank you for convincing Jake to finally get those X rays?" She gave Beth a bear hug. "How did you do it?"

"I don't know. I just reasoned with him, I guess."

Emily released Beth but reached for both of her hands and held them. "That can't be it. Jake doesn't listen to reason. It must be you, my dear. He seems quite fond of you."

Beth's cheeks grew warm. "I-I like him too."

Emily's smile grew wider. "You're good for him. He likes Kevin a lot too."

They heard a *clip-clop* and looked to see Jake leading two horses. One was Thunder with his four recognizable white socks. The other horse was a chestnut color.

Emily dropped Beth's hands and turned to Jake. "Try and have some fun on the trip."

"At the hospital? That seems unlikely." Jake gave her a peck on the cheek.

"Take your time. Take Beth out for a nice supper, too. Hear?"

"Good idea," Jake said, handing Thunder's reins to Beth.

"I have to tell Kevin that we're leaving," she said.

"I told him. He said to have a good time," Jake replied.

Beth chuckled. "That's it?"

"That's it. Kevin is mesmerized by Clint's stories. After they sing 'Buffalo Gals,' which only Clint knows the words to, he'll be telling another story—something about a ghost in mine shaft twenty-nine."

"Kids love their ghost stories, but I should go and remind Clint not to make it too scary," Emily said. "Now, you two have a good time."

"At the hospital?" Jake repeated.

"On the whole trip," Emily said. "Drive carefully!"

"You sure you can handle things?" Jake asked.

Emily waved them away. "There are more than enough volunteers. You just think of yourself right now. You're hurting with every step you take."

With five hops, Beth was up in the saddle. "I don't know why men don't listen to us women. Haven't they figured out that we're always right?"

Emily laughed. "True. So true."

"Ha!" Jake said. "You've both mastered the art of nagging. I'm going just so I don't have to listen to you both anymore."

"Whatever it takes," said Emily.

The three-hour drive to the hospital seemed short. Jake pointed out mule deer and elk, but the highlight of the trip was a herd of pronghorns at full sprint across the flatlands.

They made small talk, and Beth sensed that Jake was a little nervous about what he might find out at the hospital.

"They probably won't tell you anything today," she assured him. "The technicians will have to read the X rays and write up a report for Dr. Trotter. It'll be a few days."

"You don't know Trot. It'll be a couple of hours."

As they drove, she got to know him better. She loved to listen to him talk. He had just the right amount of country in his deep, rich voice. He was one sexy man, and she could understand why the buckle bunnies flocked around him.

She asked him questions about the terrain and cows and bulls, and he answered them with the utmost patience and a touch of humor.

When they arrived they parked in the garage adjacent to the hospital and walked into the main lobby. The candy striper blowing bubble gum behind the desk immediately recognized Jake.

"Jake Dixon!" She popped up out of her chair. "I just love you."

"Thank you." Jake's eyes glittered with humor.

"What are you doing here?" Her gum snapped. "You okay, Jake?"

"I'm fine. Just going to get some pictures taken. Can you point me towards the X-ray Department?"

She pointed. "Follow the blue line on the wall until it changes to the green line. Take the green line to the elevator. Take the elevator to the third floor. Then follow the purple line to red. Then you'll see it on the right. Yellow door."

Beth raised an eyebrow. "Blue, green, elevator to three, red, purple, yellow door. Right?"

"No. Purple then red." Her eyes never left Jake.

"What's the room number?"

She looked at Beth and rolled her eyes. "Three-twenty-two."

Jake tweaked his hat to her. "Thank you."

Beth felt Jake's hand at the small of her back as he walked her toward the blue line. She liked it.

His boots clicked against the polished marble floor. Her sneakers squawked like crows.

They found the X-ray Department, only having to ask four people to direct them. While Jake signed in, Beth found a rack of magazines and shuffled through them until she saw a pair of familiar blue eyes staring at her. She pulled out the magazine.

"Jake, your picture's on the cover," she said, holding it up to show him.

He held out his hand and she gave it to him. "It's a rag. Why don't you read something else?"

"I'd like to read this one, since it's about you."

He rolled it up and smacked it against his leg. "I'd really appreciate it if you read something else."

"I presume they said something about you that you don't want me to see." She shrugged. "Okay."

They called his name and he took the magazine with him.

"Darn," she mumbled.

With a shrug, Jake turned around and handed her back the magazine. "Go ahead, but remember, don't believe everything you read."

Beth got comfortable in the chair and found the article.

Jake Dixon: Should He Retire Or Ride?

Jake Dixon of Mountain Springs, Wyoming, has won just about every Gold Buckle worth winning, but it's a coin toss whether or not Jake will make it to Las Vegas this October for the Professional Bull Riders (PBR) Finals. At the time of writing, Dixon is ranked thirty-fifth out of forty-five bull riders, and he's currently nursing a groin, leg and back injury.

To add insult to his injuries, Viking Farm Tractors and Master Pro Tools have withdrawn their sponsorship. Instead they are sponsoring Wade Cord, the number-two ranked bull rider.

We understand that Jake Dixon wants to go out on top, but we don't want to see him permanently injured. He's given a lot to the sport, but let's face it, he's a great-granddaddy in a sport of young buckaroos....

The rest of the article was more of the same. So she skipped it and looked at the pictures of Jake being stepped on by White Whale, being tossed in the air by Grand Slam, and being rolled on the dirt by the nose of Mighty Max.

Why would anyone want to be a bull rider?

The door opened and a nurse appeared. She had a friendly smile and a scrubbed, shiny face, with teeth as white as her uniform. A tiny woman, she had an air of authority about her.

"You must be Beth."

Beth nodded.

"I'm Shirley. Mr. Dixon will be a little longer. Dr. Trotter called. He said that while we have Jake captive, he might as well order more tests." She laughed. "And Jake is in there hooting and hollering like he's being hog-tied."

Beth smiled. "I can just imagine."

"No sense hanging around here, honey. Why don't you go to the cafeteria and have a bite to eat? I'll have him meet you there."

"Thank you, Shirley. I think I'll do that."

"First floor, rear. Follow the purple line until..." Shirley shook her head. "Forget it. Go to the first floor. Today's special is tuna-noodle casserole. Just follow the smell."

Beth found the elevator and hit the button to the first floor, but made a wrong turn somewhere. She walked on, figuring she'd find a purple line somewhere. Seeing some people ahead, she decided she'd ask them for directions.

As she approached, she heard a child crying as medical staff scurried about. Straight ahead was a wall of windows and doors. She could see an ambulance parked outside, and EMTs rolling a stretcher from it, then hurrying through the big glass doors into the Emergency Room.

A young boy lay on the stretcher. He was covered in blood. Next to him, a young woman was crying, saying his name over and over. "Johnny...Johnny... Johnny...I'm here. Mommy's here, Johnny."

Beth pressed her back to the wall. She watched through the windows on her right as Johnny was wheeled to the back of the Emergency Room.

She couldn't move, couldn't swallow the lump that formed in her throat. She flashed back to two years ago. *"Kevin...Kevin... It's Mommy, Kevin. Mommy's here, Kevin."* She closed her eyes and let the tears come.

"Are you okay, miss?"

Beth opened her eyes to see an elderly woman with a Volunteer name tag pinned to her bright red lab jacket. She stuffed some tissues into Beth's hand.

"Can I help?"

Beth shook her head and sniffed. "I'm okay. I'm just thinking…thinking back to another time."

"Follow me."

Beth didn't know why, but she followed the woman as instructed. It must have been something in her kindly eyes, or the way she reminded Beth of her boss Inez.

"This is our meditation room." She flicked on a dim light. "No one's here. You relax now, dear." She left quickly, probably sensing that Beth didn't want to talk.

Beth sank into one of the overstuffed chairs and looked around. There was a mural of a water scene on the front wall. To the right of the mural was a fountain, a girl and a boy under an umbrella. Water was trickling down the umbrella into the bowl of the fountain. The sound of the water was soothing. A couple of bushes, probably silk, flanked the fountain.

Beth sat in the chair, feeling drained. She said a prayer for Johnny, then another for Kevin, and another for all the kids who were sick and suffering in the world. Children, the innocent and yet the bravest and most resilient of us all.

She didn't know how long she had been sitting there with her eyes closed, listening to the water trickling, when she felt a hand on her shoulder. She jumped.

"I'm sorry. I didn't mean to scare you." Jake's voice was a whisper, as if he were in church.

She took his hand. She wanted some connection with this man, brave in his own way. A man fighting his own battles.

"How did you find me?"

"My friend the candy striper saw you go this way. Then I asked one of the volunteers in the hallway, and she knew you right off."

He took a seat next to her. In the dim light, she could barely see him, but she could smell his aftershave. Could hear his steady breathing.

"Are you all right?"

"I had some kind of a meltdown, Jake. I saw a young boy being wheeled into the ER and it reminded me of the day of the accident. All I could see was Kevin covered in blood and..."

He took her hand, and she felt a connection to him, a warmness that started in her heart and spread over her like a warm blanket. She looked at their hands clasped together. It seemed so natural to confide in him, to share what was in her soul.

"It's my fault that Kevin's in a wheelchair. I didn't know that Brad had started drinking again. I should have known. I should have known, Jake."

He put an arm around her shoulder. She leaned into him.

"It wasn't your fault. It was Brad's fault."

"I wish I could believe that."

"Believe it."

"I hate it when I'm like this. I feel...weak."

"Weak? So, you're not allowed to show any emotion? You have to keep it all in, to be brave?"

"Yes."

"You've dealt with the death of your husband and the almost death and long rehabilitation of your son. Plus, you blame yourself for the accident, for not knowing that Brad was drinking again. Let's see, what else can we load on your shoulders?"

She smiled and squeezed his hand.

"Jake Dixon, you're good for me." Beth felt the fog lifting from her brain. She wiped her tears and blew her nose. She took a couple of deep breaths and felt better. "How did you make out in X-ray Land?"

"I was stripped naked and posed and photographed from every angle. That idiot Trot even ordered blood tests!"

"Did you wear one of those gowns that open in the back?"

"Yup."

"Wish I could have seen that." She chuckled. "And I'll bet you never took off your boots or your hat."

"They made me take off my boots, but I never took off my hat."

"And you only take your hat off for one thing and one thing only."

He slapped his knee. "How did you know that, darlin'?" He went heavy on the western accent.

"I think we're doing the dialogue from a bad western movie, *darlin'*." Beth felt better. He was good for her. "Shall we go?"

"You okay now?"

"Yes. Thanks."

"Beth?" His voice was low, a whisper on the air.

He pulled her into his arms. His index finger traced her lips and the side of her jaw. Beth was glad that the chair was behind her in case she fell, because her knees weren't locking.

He bent his head and kissed her. When his tongue traced her lips, she sighed, opened for him. He held her tighter. She took off his cowboy hat and ran her fingers through his soft hair.

She let herself feel—the touch of his callused hands on her arms, the softness of his lips, the way his breath caressed her face when he spoke her name.

What was she doing? She broke the kiss, astonished by the way he made her feel. He'd kissed her before, but she wasn't ready for this—this intense feeling for him.

She couldn't get involved with a man who might have a drinking problem. A man who could end up in a wheelchair like Kevin because of his injuries. A man who rode bulls, one of the most dangerous sports of all, so much so that being wheeled from an ambulance into the Emergency Room was routine.

"Jake, I'm going to talk to Johnny's mother. Maybe I can just hold her hand and keep her company or get her some water or something. Do you mind?"

"Not at all."

He smiled at her, a smile that told her that he admired her.

"Are you sure you can handle it?" he asked.

"I think so. I'm okay now."

"Then you go right ahead, and take your time."

Chapter Nine

Jake crossed his arms and ankles and leaned against the wall in the hallway. Through the thick glass window across from him, he could see the waiting area of the Emergency Room.

It looked like every other emergency room he'd been in, and he'd been in many. If he couldn't be stitched or taped at the sports medicine office, he'd be strapped to a stretcher and slipped into an ambulance like a letter into an envelope. Then he'd be rushed to the nearest hospital.

When it was one of his fellow bull riders who took a bad hit, he'd drive over to the hospital after the event to keep him company.

If things weren't that bad, they'd hit the road and head to the next event.

Yep. ERs were all the same—crowded with barely

enough uncomfortable plastic chairs for everyone. Some people paced, others sat as still as statues. Some cried softly, others looked ever hopeful as they waited for news.

The broken and bloody were the ones Jake identified with. They'd have to wait, sometimes hours, before their names were called. He'd experienced that too many times.

Beth sat next to a young woman who he assumed was Johnny's mother. They were talking intently. Beth had her arm around the woman's shoulder, and they held hands in a fisted grip.

Jake knew it had to be hard on Beth to experience Kevin's accident all over again. Yet she was there for a stranger who was going through the same thing, supporting her, caring.

Beth Conroy was one special woman.

She didn't have to drive with him to the hospital. He could have gone for X rays another time. Maybe after the Challenge was over. But she sure was persuasive. No. It wasn't just that. It was because he wanted to be with her—alone—and away from all the distractions back at the ranch.

When they kissed, he felt something stir inside his very soul. Sure, he had the normal physical jolt, but there was more, like the adrenaline rush when he won a Gold Buckle or rode a bull that no one else could.

He'd noticed her doing little things around the ranch to help—she talked to the kids, wiped tables, served meals and pitched in generally. She could have taken a break, like many of the parents did, but she was always willing to lend a hand.

He didn't begrudge the parents some time by

themselves while the kids were participating in the program. It was hard being the caretaker for someone with special needs. He could see the exhaustion on their faces, in their eyes, in the slump of their shoulders.

Beth had had that same look of exhaustion when he'd picked her and Kevin up at the airport. Now it seemed almost gone.

For the time she had left at the Gold Buckle, he wanted to show her a good time. Last night's adventure at the Last Chance Saloon had had its highs and lows, but now he knew the mistake he'd made.

He drank in front of Beth.

Jake noticed a doctor-type dressed in aqua-colored scrubs enter the waiting room through big steel double doors. Everyone turned in his direction and held a collective breath, until he picked out the person he was looking for. Beth's new friend stood, gave a solemn nod and disappeared behind the doors after the doctor.

With her hands folded in her lap, Beth looked around. Her gaze settled on Jake. She smiled. He smiled back and waved, then waited as he watched her walk from the glass room toward him.

"Her name is Maria," she said. "Johnny was riding his bicycle home from baseball practice and a woman driver talking on a cell phone hit him. Maria is with the doctor who examined Johnny now." Beth's breath came out in a shudder. "I hope he'll be all right."

"I hope so, too."

"Jake, I know you're anxious to go back to the ranch, but would you mind if I just stay a little longer with

Maria? She might need someone to talk to, and I'd like to be here for her."

"Like I said, you take all the time you need." He pointed outside. "I'll be out there. There's a garden with a couple of benches. Sure you don't want to take a break and catch some air?"

Looking back at the room, she shook her head. "In case Maria needs a shoulder to cry on, I want to be there."

"Then you go right ahead."

She gave him a quick peck on the cheek. Nice. He'd rope the moon for her whenever she looked at him like that with those big green eyes. Hell, he'd camp out in the garden all night if she wanted to stay in the ER with Maria.

"Thanks, Jake."

He watched as she walked away, her blond hair catching glints from the overhead lights and her stride purposeful. As he watched her take a seat through the glass wall of the waiting room, his mind strayed, thinking of how she'd felt in his arms as they'd danced last night. How she'd responded to his kisses at her cabin door, in the meadow, in the chapel…

He couldn't help thinking that they were on some kind of journey together, each hesitant to take another step, yet each wondering what was over the next ridge.

Someone called to him. "Jake? Hey, Jake!"

Looking down, he saw two of the cutest kids, a boy and a girl. The boy was about seven, the girl about four or five.

He looked around to see if any adults were looking for them. Behind the glass of the ER, a woman pointed to the children and then to herself. Jake nodded.

"Hey, Jake!" the boy said again. "Can we have your autograph?"

"Why sure, son. What's your name?"

"Guillermo Hernandez-Rodriguez. And I'm gonna be a bull rider just like you."

"Be better than me," Jake told him.

The boy thrust a pen and a colorful rectangle of paper at Jake, who bit back a laugh. It was a magazine subscription form that little Guillermo must have found in the stacks of magazines in the waiting room.

"You're probably going to have to spell your name for me so I can get it right."

"Um…naw, just write 'Billy' on it. It's spelled B-I-L-L-Y."

Jake had just finished the N in Dixon, when Billy pulled the paper out of his hand and ran off. Jake watched through the window as Billy showed it to his mother. She smiled her appreciation to Jake, and he touched his hat to her.

Jake turned toward Beth. She was watching him, smiling.

He felt a push on his leg. "Hey! Me, too!"

Awkwardly, Jake crouched down to be eye to eye with the little girl. "And what's your name, princess?"

"Theresa Hernandez-Rodriguez, and this is a new dress. It's pink." She twirled in a complete circle twice, then ended up facing him. "I want to be a ballerina."

"I think you'd make an excellent ballerina," Jake said. This little gal was just perfection. "And your dress is beautiful on you."

She stuck her chin out and grinned. She had some teeth missing and some starting to come in.

"Do you want me to write 'Theresa' on this paper?"

She nodded, then spun around again. Jake held back his laughter.

"What's your name again, mister?" she asked.

"Jake. Jake Dixon."

"Oh." She twirled so fast this time that she spun, fell, her bottom hitting the marble floor. Her eyes shot open wide and her bottom lip trembled, but she seemed to be more shocked than hurt.

Oh hell, she was going to cry. It broke his heart when kids cried. "Are you okay, Theresa?" He helped her up. "That was a great spin, but maybe a little too fast. Ballerinas dance really slow." How would he know? It wasn't as if he'd ever seen a ballet in his life.

To her credit, no tears fell. She looked at her dress, smoothed it down and was back to her old self.

Jake knew she didn't have a clue as to why he was writing on a magazine subscription card for her.

"My daddy's hurt."

He chose his words carefully. "The doctors are going to take good care of him," he said, struggling to stand. His legs were numb and it felt like his back wasn't going to lock into place.

"A bull got him."

"A bull?" Jake said a quick prayer. This could be bad for her father.

Theresa cupped her mouth with both hands and whispered, "A bull's horns got him in the butt."

He covered his mouth, ostensibly rubbing his chin. He shouldn't laugh. He just shouldn't. But he was relieved for her father that the injury probably wasn't life threatening. Then it hit him.

"Is your daddy's name Miguel?"

She nodded.

"And you have a big ranch and lot of bulls, don't you?"

She nodded. "And horses. My horse's name is Candy, and Daddy says he's as sweet as me."

Big Mike Rodriguez was one of the most important rodeo stock contractors in the country. He was a short, square, hulk of a man with a heart as big as his best bull, Tiny Tim. He was a wealthy, self-made man who gave buckets of money to Wheelchair Rodeo.

"I know your daddy."

"You do?" Theresa took him by the hand and tugged.

"Where are you taking me, princess?"

"I want to show you to my daddy."

"But he's busy right now. You just show him what I wrote on that paper and tell him I said to get better, okay?" When this got around the circuit, Big Mike Rodriguez would be the butt of a lot of jokes. Jake groaned at his own pun.

"Theresa, come now. You've bothered Mr. Dixon long enough."

"Hi, Mommy!" Theresa twirled back to her mother, then curtseyed to him with a bit too much of her pink dress gathered into her hands.

Jake bowed to Theresa as much as his back would let him, then tweaked the brim of his hat. She giggled and took another bow.

"She's no problem," he said to Mrs. Rodriguez. "I've enjoyed talking to her. I'm Jake Dixon." He held his hand out.

"Kathleen." She shook his hand. "I think we met a while back."

He didn't remember. "Theresa tells me that Big Mike was hurt. Sure hope he'll be okay."

"He'll be fine. Just needs a couple dozen stitches. I'm sure Theresa told you on what part of his anatomy he needs them." She laughed. "She's telling everyone."

Jake grinned. "Please tell Big Mike I said hello and that I'll pass the word as to what happened to him."

"I think that's what Mike was afraid of!" She held on to Theresa's shoulders, probably to still her before she twirled right into Colorado. "I hope you're all right yourself, Jake."

"Oh, I'm okay. Just had some X rays. Right now I'm waiting on a friend who's keeping someone company."

He pointed to Beth, who must have been watching him all along. He met her gaze and knew her warm smile was for him. That made him feel good right down to the soles of his boots.

After more small talk, Theresa and her mother went back inside and Jake headed out to the garden.

He collapsed on one of the benches and thought about how he'd love to have kids of his own someday. But when was "someday" going to come? He wasn't ready to give up riding. Some riders combined a family life with rodeo, but that wasn't for him. He wouldn't like being gone from his family that much. Some dragged their families with them, but what kind of a life was that for children?

Interacting with the kids was the main reason he enjoyed Wheelchair Rodeo so much. For one week in July, it seemed as though they were all his kids, and he could enjoy each and every one of them.

Since he never wore a watch, he checked the position of the sun in the sky. Although he didn't want to rush Beth, he couldn't wait to get back to the ranch. Tonight was movie night, which usually turned into a laugh-fest and a popcorn fight. He had a John Wayne movie ready to roll. Lights-out would be at nine o'clock. They were going to get an early start on the trail ride tomorrow, and he wanted everyone fresh and alert.

He shifted his weight on the hard bench and ran through a list in his head. Everything was set for tomorrow's campout, and Jake was looking forward to it.

As Beth walked toward Jake, she couldn't help thinking how cute he had been with the two little autograph seekers. She'd watched him work his magic with them, just as he'd worked his magic with Kevin and Heather, the little girl who'd wanted a golden horse instead of a gray one. The kids in Wheelchair Rodeo adored him. Kevin idolized him.

"Mommy, he said I was a princess."

"Hey, Mom, I'm going to be a bull rider like Jake Dixon."

Jake had a way about him that made a person feel special. Like the way he made her feel when she was with him.

He had his face turned up to the sun, and his eyes were shut. His arms were crossed in front of his chest, and he was stretched out. He looked peaceful and relaxed, and she wondered what he was thinking.

She cleared her throat, and his turquoise eyes opened slowly.

He patted the bench next to him. "Any news?"

She sat down. "The good news is that Johnny's going to be okay—eventually. His most serious injury is a fractured pelvis, so they are going to put in pins and metal plates." She sighed. "Kevin had a fractured pelvis too, among other things."

Jake put his arm around her shoulders and pulled her closer. She let her head rest on his chest, taking comfort from him, drawing on his strength.

She'd never had anyone to share life's daily struggles with, and wondered if it would feel like this. Marriage was supposed to be like this but what a disappointment hers had been. It had been next to impossible to share her life with Brad; he was always drunk or hungover. They never hugged or kissed, and forget about sex. If he did show up in their bed, he was sleeping off a bender.

She found herself getting all warm and tingly when she thought of making love with Jake. She wanted to know what it would be like with him—just once. One wonderful time.

"Thanks for not rushing me. It was something I had to do."

"I know." He squeezed her hand. "It was a nice thing you did. I know it was hard."

She sighed as peace and contentment washed over her. She would remember this moment forever when she was back in Arizona—sitting here on a bench in Wyoming with Jake's strong arm around her. Her heart ached with admiration for him.

"Jake?"

"Hmm?"

"When did we cross the line between friendship and more than friendship?"

"I haven't a clue."

She could feel the vibration in his chest as he spoke.

"Only a couple of days ago, you couldn't stand the sight of me."

"Not true. You're gorgeous to look at, but you know I hate drinking."

He chuckled. "Gorgeous, huh?"

She coughed. "Absolutely."

"Studly?"

She put her tongue against her cheek. "You got it."

"Sexy?"

She rolled her eyes. "Goes without saying." Her stomach growled. "Shall we go back to the Gold Buckle?"

"Let's talk more about me."

She moved away from him and stood, faking like she was upset. "I'm not one of your buckle bunnies, Jake Dixon."

"Gee, too bad. If you were, I'd autograph your stomach."

"No thanks, but you can feed it. I'm famished."

He attempted to stand, using the bench for leverage. Automatically, she moved to help him, the way she always helped Kevin.

"No. I can do it myself. It just takes time."

She opened her mouth to protest, but he cut her off.

"I promised my mother that I'd take you someplace special to eat."

She thought about it. "Let's just go back to the Gold Buckle. That's someplace special to me. Besides, I heard Cookie's making sourdough biscuits and barbecuing steaks. I just love cookouts and eating outside."

"Sounds good to me."

Hand in hand, they walked back to the parking garage, and were soon back on the highway heading southwest. The sun was still high in the sky, and the sky was even bluer than on the way up.

"I gave Maria the address of the Gold Buckle Ranch for Johnny. I told her about your program and how it's done so much for Kevin."

"Great," Jake replied. "If there's anything I can do for them…"

She heard a phone ringing somewhere in the truck.

"Try the glove compartment. I forgot I had the thing."

She answered the phone for him. "It's Owen Michaelson from Wild West Pro Rodeo Equipment."

"Tell him to hang on."

Jake turned in to a gas station, cut the motor and took the phone. "Hi, Owen. How's everything?"

His shoulders slumped as he answered in one-word sentences. Beth sensed that it wasn't good news.

"I wish you'd give me more time, but I understand. Chris Morton is a good man. He's going places. Do what you have to, Owen. Okay."

He handed her the phone. "Thank you."

She put it back where she had found it. "Something wrong?"

"Lost another sponsor."

Beth didn't know what to say. The article she'd read earlier had mentioned that he'd lost two previously. This made three.

"Do you have any sponsors left?"

"Nothing big."

She wished she could think of something to lessen

his disappointment. "Well, look at the bright side. You're still gorgeous, studly and sexy, and you can autograph my stomach anytime you want."

He laughed, but they rode back to the Gold Buckle Ranch mostly in silence. No matter how hard she tried to get him to open up, he shrugged the news off as if it didn't matter—but she knew it did.

She sensed that he wanted to be alone, so she was glad when she started seeing signs for Mountain Springs.

He swung his truck into the parking area marked "Visitors." "Thanks for keeping me company," he said as they got out of the truck.

"It was my pleasure. Thanks for the shoulder to lean on. Wish I could have done the same for you when you got that call."

"You did."

She shut the door. "You aren't the easiest to get to open up about yourself, but you are a pro at getting others to open up to you."

He opened the passenger door that Beth had just shut and took out the cell phone. For a second he looked at it as if trying to decide if he should throw the phone as far as he could or crush it under his boot. The sparkle seemed to have left his eyes.

"Jake?" She touched his arm. "Are you going to be all right?"

"Yeah."

"I'm worried that you might…"

He raised a dark eyebrow. "Worried that I might go out and get drunk and get into another brawl?" His words were sarcastic and biting. "You will never stop comparing me to your ex-husband, will you."

She stepped back, stung by the words she knew were true. "I'm trying. I'm really trying."

He caught her hand and took a deep breath. "I'm fine. Don't worry about me. Jake Dixon has been stomped on before and survived. Okay?"

"I'm sorry. It's not fair of me."

"No apology necessary."

He was right, she had to stop comparing him to Brad.

Jake checked his watch. "I'd better go check on a couple of things, so I'll see you later at the cookout."

"Okay."

She'd planned on a quick nap before the barbecue, but she wanted to see Kevin first to tell him that she was back. She walked toward the horse barn. If he was anywhere, he was probably feeding or watering the horses.

Entering the barn, she inhaled the smell of horses, sweet hay and leather. Sure enough, Kevin was talking to another boy in a wheelchair. They were feeding carrots to all horses that were sticking their heads over the half-doors, which most of them were.

She waved to the three cowboys cleaning tack, and they waved back.

"Hey, Mom!" Kevin waved to her with a carrot in his hand.

Carrots were always in his hands lately, and he was always in the horse barn, riding a horse or talking about horses.

"Where's Jake?" he asked.

"He's around. How are you, Kevin? Having fun?"

"Sure am." Then he remembered his manners. "This is Luke. Luke, this is my mom."

"Hi, Luke." She shook his hand. "Nice to meet you."

"Howdy, ma'am," he replied.

"Mom, Luke's from Stephenville, Texas. Doesn't he talk cool? We're going to e-mail each other when Wheelchair Rodeo is over. His horse is named Super Dude. Isn't that a cool name?"

"Cool."

"Is Jake going to be okay?" Kevin asked.

"They took a lot of X rays. Then Dr. Trotter will look at them and talk to Jake."

"Hope he's okay."

"Me too."

"Me three," added Luke.

"Are you going to be at the movie, Mom? It's a John Wayne one. Lots of shootin' and stuff."

"I'll be there." She wanted to kiss him and give him a big hug, but she didn't dare with Luke or the other cowboys in the barn. Kevin would never forgive her. "I'll see you later, then."

To her surprise, Kevin turned to Luke and told him that he could continue to feed the horses without him because he was going to "escort" his mother part of the way back to her cabin. She wondered what was up, and hoped something wasn't wrong.

Kevin waited until they were down the ramp and away from everyone. His eyes took in the area. No one was around. "Mom, you can hug me if you want to. You can kiss me, too."

"Aw..." She bent over and did just that. He hugged her back. "How did you know I needed that?"

"I just thought you did."

She kissed him on the forehead. "I'm feeling better

already." She mussed his hair, and he didn't protest. Was this boy actually Kevin? "But are you okay?"

He shifted in his seat as if he couldn't get comfortable. "Um, yeah…I'm okay."

She'd bet her last dollar that something was on his mind. "Anything you want to tell me?"

"Uh, well, remember how after my last operation I was supposed to walk?"

She squatted and took his hands. "Yes, but don't worry, honey. Maybe you just need more time."

Some cowboys walked past them. They all waved and called Kevin by name. He knew their names, too.

"Was there something more you wanted to tell me, Kev?"

His gaze followed the cowboys as they walked away. "Uh, nope. I don't think so."

"Okay."

She was striking out. Her kid was secretive and so was Jake Dixon—but she knew her son better than she did Jake Dixon. Something was up with Kevin, only he wasn't ready to talk about it yet. He was just laying the foundation.

"See you later, Mom."

"See you at the barbecue."

Pushing open the door to her cabin, she went to her refrigerator and pulled out a can of iced tea. Taking a couple of swigs, she went into her bedroom, put the can on the night table and collapsed onto the bed.

She just wanted to close her eyes, just for a moment.

Jake wondered why Beth had missed the barbecue. He really began to worry when Kevin came to him and told him that the John Wayne movie had started and his mother still wasn't there.

"But she said that she was going to be at the movie, Jake. She said she would." He began to wheel rapidly toward the exit.

"Hey, Kev, you stay here and find out what The Duke does to get the bad guys, and I'll go check on your mother. I'm sure she's fine. She's probably just sleeping."

"Thanks."

He handed Kevin a cell phone. "I'll call you when I've talked to her. You just stay and have fun."

"Call me. Right away."

"You got it."

There were no lights on in the Trail Boss Cabin. Jake knocked on the door. "Beth?"

No answer.

"Beth?"

Still no answer.

He walked in and turned a light on in the living room. He walked down the hallway and paused at the bedroom door. She was curled up on her side, sound asleep. She had unbuttoned her blouse and loosened the top snap of her shorts. Her hair was a mass of gold on the pillow, and she was breathing in soft little puffs.

He debated whether he should wake her. She hadn't had anything to eat, and, heaven forbid, she was missing a John Wayne movie.

He walked back into the living room and dialed his cell phone. "Kev? It's Jake. Your mom is in the cabin. She's sleeping, so we'll let her be. Obviously, she doesn't like The Duke as much as the rest of us."

"Will you come back to the movie, Jake? It's really cool," asked Kevin.

Jake could hear the noise around Kevin. Typical movie night. No one watched the movie, and then there would be the inevitable popcorn fight.

"I'll see you in the morning. I have some things to do. Get a good night's rest."

"Okay, Jake."

He turned and walked back into the bedroom. He had an overwhelming urge to taste Beth's lips again.

Chapter Ten

Beth was half awake when she heard Jake talking to Kevin, or maybe she was dreaming.

She'd had the same dream countless times since their arrival at the ranch. Jake would stand silhouetted in the bedroom door, and she'd be lying in bed. Then he'd slowly walk over and stare down at her, his lips curving into a warm and sensuous smile. He'd bend over and briefly touch his lips to hers. She'd shiver in anticipation of more to come.

She'd look into his turquoise eyes....

Her eyes shot open. "Jake?"

He looked down at her. "I couldn't resist kissing you."

"I'm not complaining," she said, her voice breathless and her lips tingling.

Heaven help her, she wanted him to kiss her again.

He stepped closer and skimmed her cheek with his knuckles. His thumb traced her lips.

"Beth?" His voice was low and rough.

With that one word, he asked a million questions.

She knew what he wanted, but making love with Jake would complicate things, cause her to let her guard down.

Even though it'd be a bad idea, she wanted to be held by him, to feel loved and cherished and desired—feelings she hadn't experienced in a long time.

It had been forever since she'd been with her husband, and she hadn't had a date since his death. She was always too busy to think about anything or anyone other than Kevin.

"*Kevin!* I need to—"

"He's okay," Jake said. "He was worried about you when you didn't show up at the barbecue and the movie, but I just called him and told him you were sleeping. He's all set with John Wayne, a big bowl of popcorn and his pals."

What Jake had left unsaid was that they wouldn't be disturbed.

She didn't know what made her get up from the bed and stand next to him. She clasped the side of his hat brim with her thumb and index finger. "I remember you told me that this hat comes off for one thing only."

He grinned. "Do I leave it on or take it off?"

She hesitated, running her fingers along the brim, feeling its softness. She could think of only one reason why she should make love with Jake—she wanted to.

She wanted to be with this man who gave so much of himself. She felt her own need rising to the surface.

Gently, she pressed her lips to his, then said, "Take it off."

With one quick motion, he tossed his hat onto the seat of a chair and pulled her to him. His lips locked on hers, and she felt the heat building inside her, inside him. She felt the promise of things to come.

She yanked on his shirt and heard the metallic *ping* of snaps coming undone. The palms of her hands covered the hard planes of his chest, moving over his warm skin.

He was already rock hard. She could feel him through their clothes.

"Are you sure you know what you're doing?" he asked, taking her hands in his and moving to sit on the bed.

She hoped he couldn't feel her hands shaking. "Well, it's been a long time."

He chuckled, a low rumbling in his chest. "That's not what I meant."

Standing in front of him, her hands fisted in his shirt, she undid the rest of his snaps. Even in the dim light of the cabin, she could see the scars on his chest. She traced them with a finger, wishing she could erase the permanent proof that he lived dangerously.

"You know, if we stopped to think, we wouldn't do this," he said, threading his fingers through her hair.

"I already thought about it. I want to be with you."

His eyes never left hers as he shrugged out of his shirt and tossed it on the floor.

Her palms explored the hardness of his chest and back as she trailed kisses in their wake. Her hand lingered on a roughened area under his ribs above the waistband of his jeans.

"Jake?" She knelt in front of him to get a better look and saw horrific scarring about the size of her hand.

"Pretty bad, huh?" he asked. "Sorry, I should have warned you."

The pain he must have felt… She hated to see his beautiful body marred like that. "What—?"

"A bull by the name of Gentle Breeze got a little playful with me in Houston. Don't worry about it. It was years ago." He took Beth's hands and helped her to her feet. "Take your blouse off," he whispered.

She hesitated, suddenly feeling anxious. "I've only been with one man in my life, and that was my husband. We…well, it's been a long time. Years."

"Then I'll help you make up for lost time." He positioned her on his lap and covered her mouth with his. Their tongues moved in slow rhythm.

Reaching for the buttons on her blouse, he popped them open one by one. He took his time, and her anticipation only added to her excitement.

He pushed the straps of her bra off her shoulders, peeled it down. She unhooked it and let it drop, never taking her eyes off him.

He let his gaze linger on her breasts. "Beautiful," he said.

He played with a nipple, making it harden, making her squirm and moan softly. Then he cupped one breast with a large hand that looked dark against the white of her skin.

She gasped. "Mmm…I want to see you, too," she whispered. "All of you."

She unhooked his belt, and the huge oval-shaped buckle fell to the side. "Let me," she ordered, her fingers at the metal button of his jeans. Slowly, she unzipped him, link by metal link. She smiled. "I knew you'd be wearing standard white underwear."

His eyes twinkled in amusement. "You've thought about my underwear?"

Oh heavens, what had made her tell him that? "I confess. I have. Let's take them off, shall we?"

"I'm all yours, if you don't mind giving me a little help here."

With a gasp, she moved away from him. "Oh no! I forgot your injuries. Your leg…your back. I didn't think!"

"Get yourself back here, I'm fine. And there's more than one way to make love. We'll figure it out."

"Wait a minute. Let me see your leg."

"This is strange foreplay," he said, his eyes glittering.

Beth chuckled nervously, but Jake's easy smile and twinkling eyes soon had relaxed her. She watched as he pulled off his boots and slid out of his jeans, thinking how the simple gestures seemed so masculine when he did them.

When he lay back down, he held out his hand, and she joined him. She ran her hand over his hard stomach, his well-muscled thighs. His chest was smooth, powerful and bronzed by the sun.

He put an arm around her, and she was content to lie next to him, to inhale his scent, and to let her hand roam over the tough-yet-sweet cowboy next to her.

She knew he was giving her time to get comfortable, and she loved him for that.

Her lips met his, lightly and gently, and he closed his

eyes. "Mmm…" he said, with a look of contentment on his face.

He took her hand, raised it to his lips and kissed it. "If you're having second thoughts, it's best you tell me now."

She knew she wanted him, and he wanted her. She wanted to feel his hands touching her everywhere. She wanted to feel him inside her.

She wanted to *feel.*

"I'm not having second thoughts, Jake." She looked deep into his eyes and smiled.

He gathered her in his arms and kissed her hard and long. "Mmm…this is nice," he said.

As he kissed her neck and she stretched to give him more access, her nervousness was forgotten. All she could think about was this man and what he was doing to her, how he made her feel.

Beth cupped him with her hands but it wasn't enough. She wanted to feel his warm skin pulsing in her hands, feel his power. Beth couldn't believe how daring she had become, but she tugged off his underwear, then tossed it toward the rest of the clothes strewn about the floor.

Her days at the Gold Buckle were dwindling. She didn't know when she'd be alone with him again. She had to know what it was like to make love with Jake.

By the light of the moon she stared down at the man she'd come to love.

Yes, she loved him. She didn't know how or when it had happened, but she had a feeling it started back when Kevin was in the hospital and she read him articles about Jake.

She had found herself looking through bookstores

and magazine racks hoping to find the latest news about him, his latest venture, or what movie star, rodeo queen or singer he was dating. She'd read those articles alone in her room at night. Kevin couldn't have cared less about that kind of thing. Kev had just wanted his rodeo stats.

Beth had wanted his personal stats.

Yet never in her most secret of dreams had she ever expected to meet Jake Dixon in person, or lie naked with him in the Trail Boss Cabin in the middle of Wyoming.

His arms were strong, bulging with muscles, especially his riding arm. His stomach was flat with a light down of soft hair that became thicker and coarser as she explored lower. Her hand circled the length of him and she felt him throb.

They quickly dispensed with the rest of her clothes, Jake kissing her everywhere with such exquisite tenderness, it brought tears to her eyes. He held her tight, and she felt him hard against her. She shivered as he lavished slow, sensuous kisses that made her toes curl. His tongue met hers again, and it felt as if she was floating… floating…

His fingers plucked at a nipple, making her squirm and moan softly.

"You're going to have to be on top, Beth," he whispered. "I can't—"

She covered the rest of his sentence with a kiss.

He produced a condom package. It didn't take him long to tear it open and sheath himself. She watched in fascination. It was a sexy thing for him to do—and to care about her like that. At least he had more sense than she did.

"Pretty sure of yourself, aren't you?" she asked, wrapping her hand around the length of him. She felt the power surging in him.

"I knew we'd make love sooner or later." He let out a deep breath.

She moved over him and took him into her, slowly…very slowly. It had been such a long time….

She closed her eyes as he took her breasts into his large, rough hands and rolled her nipples between his callused fingers.

She moved, gasping at the sensations—how deep he was inside her, how good it felt. She slid up and down the length of him, stopping only to catch her breath and to look into his blue eyes, now dark with passion.

They couldn't get enough of each other. They clung, teased, touched and kissed until the fire between them warmed the little Trail Boss Cabin.

She set the pace. Faster. His eyes closed.

He shuddered when she did, calling her name. When they each found their release, they knew it was more than just making love—it was a joining of their souls.

All too soon they drifted back to the little cabin in the pines.

Later they snuggled under the covers, Beth with her head on Jake's chest, his chin on her head.

"I feel so peaceful, Jake. Like I don't have a care in the world."

"No regrets?"

"No regrets."

There would be plenty of regrets later when she had time to think. She was leaving and she'd never see Jake Dixon again. He'd go back to riding as long as he could still climb on the back of a bull, and she'd go back to leasing apartments in Arizona.

Funny how life threw you a curveball every now and then.

Beth fell asleep in Jake's arms, for the moment, content.

"Damn! I've overslept!"

The bed rocked like a boat on a storm-tossed sea as Jake flung the covers off and tugged on his jeans.

"In ten minutes my mother will be leading the Pledge of Allegiance at the flagpole."

Beth's eyes sprang open. "Ten minutes? Ten minutes!" Everyone would be gathered around the flagpole, and the flagpole was within sight of her cabin. "Jake, you can't be seen leaving here! Kevin...your parents...the other cowboys...the kids. *Kevin!*"

She sprang out of bed and tossed on a T-shirt and a pair of shorts that she'd picked up off the floor.

"I'll go out the back porch door, but we'd both better hurry. We ride out on the trail drive right after the Cowboy/Cowgirl Prayer."

"Oh, no! I have to take a shower and pack...and... and..."

"Get a move on, then!" After giving Beth a quick kiss, Jake yanked on his jeans, gathered up his boots and stuffed his socks and underwear into them. He grabbed his shirt and hurried out the back door, limping as fast as he could down the Chisholm Trail.

Beth moved like lightning. She would have liked to linger with Jake in bed, maybe make love with him yet again, but she was committed to help with the girls. She'd be riding Thunder.

She jumped in the shower and washed her hair. She was a little stiff after using muscles that she hadn't used in ages. A shiver of excitement went through her when she thought of how they made love for a second time with her legs around his hips, Jake pressing her against the wall of the cabin....

Then again as she sat on the edge of the dresser...

They couldn't get enough of each other.

She toweled herself off and quickly dressed. Luckily, she had some items packed in a saddle bag, and it didn't take her much time to pack a sweatshirt and other items from the list that Emily had passed out earlier.

She combed her wet hair as she walked to the flagpole. She made it with time to spare. Jake arrived minutes later, tucking in his shirt and finger-combing his wet hair. He held his hat in his hand.

He gave her a big smile and moved around the edge of the crowd to stand next to her. The scent of his soap and, yes, Bull-istic, drifted on the morning breeze. He didn't shave, and that made him look sexy. She itched to run her fingers through his damp hair, to press her lips to his in the bright light of day.

She made eye contact with Kevin and waved. He waved back, a big grin on his face. She could tell that he was so excited he could barely sit still.

Emily started the Pledge of Allegiance. Dex led the "Star Spangled Banner." Then Dex said a special Cowboy/Cowgirl Prayer:

"O Great Spirit, keep everyone safe on this journey. May the spirits of the pioneers who traveled great distances to settle this great country, guide us. And may we have lots of fun."

A big cheer rose from the assembly, getting the kids even more pumped. Then it was Jake's turn for announcements. Clint Scully handed him a clipboard; Jake nodded his gratitude. No doubt he hadn't had time to prepare.

"All riders report to the barn to saddle your horse. All those on the hay wagon, bring your gear and yourselves to the lobby area. All volunteers, please see Clint Scully for your assignment. We'll all line up for the wagon train in front of the lobby. Any guests who aren't joining us, you're going to have to take your meals in town. We'll be back early tomorrow evening." Jake waved his hat in the air. "Let's go, everyone! The wagon train leaves exactly one half hour from now!"

Organized chaos ensued. There were kisses and hugs from parents. Last-minute checks on saddle bags and last-minute instructions from Em, Dex and Jake.

The cowboys scattered in various directions, each with a mission in mind.

Beth got her assignment from Clint. She was going to take care of two girls: Kathy Holmes and Marylou Doxtator. They were both riders and would be on horseback. She had talked to the girls several times. Both were just adorable.

Then she walked to the barn with Kevin.

"Mom, is this not totally cool, or what?"

"Kevin, it's totally cool."

"This is awesome, Mom. Awesome."

She laughed. "Totally awesome!"

"This is just like the pioneers, huh?"

"Absolutely." Looking around and seeing no one, she bent down. "Kevin, no one is around. Can I just give you a kiss and a hug?"

He verified that no one was around. "Okay. But hurry."

"I will."

She kissed him on the cheek and added a big hug. She could tell that he loved it, but would never admit it.

"All done, and you survived. Let's go saddle our horses."

"All right!"

Jake held his hand up and yelled, "Westward ho!"

Beth and Kevin rode next to him, something she was sure he'd arranged. She liked that. Better yet, Kevin liked it.

Her two charges, Kathy and Marylou, were behind her, content to drool over the cowboys who were riding with them.

Dex and Emily rode next, followed by Cookie driving the chuck wagon. Clint Scully rode shotgun on the chuck wagon, munching on an apple, his guitar at his side.

Next came the hay wagons with the kids who couldn't ride horses. They were with some volunteers and assorted cowboys. All had big grins.

The medical wagon was next in line. Doc Trotter drove. Beth recognized several EMTs and nurses.

Bringing up the rear was a supply wagon loaded

with tents, sleeping bags, big jugs of drinking water, feed for the horses and other items for the campout.

It was a big operation. Beth admired Jake's skill in putting it all together.

Jake put a hand on Kevin's shoulder. "Kev, can you take over being wagon master for a bit?"

Kevin nodded so hard, Beth thought he was going to fall off his horse. Jake winked at Beth, and she lost her heart completely to him in that second—the second that he made a little boy feel like the most important creature in the world. She winked back.

"Just take it slow, Wagon Master Kevin. I'm going to make sure everyone's rolling."

"Okay, Jake!" Kevin sat up taller in the saddle. He turned to Beth. "Isn't this just the coolest thing in the world, Mom? I'm a wagon master!"

"You sure are."

She couldn't resist turning back to look at Jake. He was every bit the cowboy with his boots, hat and faded jeans. His very presence commanded respect. Maybe it was the way he sat in the saddle, maybe it was just his demeanor, but whatever it was, people listened to him.

A quiver ran through her when she thought of him naked and hard. He was an attentive lover, thinking of her needs before his own. Thank goodness he had had the foresight to bring a condom or two—or three—with him.

"Mom, which way do we go?"

"I think we turn left, but I'm not sure."

She heard galloping alongside and knew it was Jake. One hand was on top of his hat, keeping it from flying off as he rode. He looked wild and western, and she wanted him again.

"Hey, Wagon Master! Go left up ahead," he yelled.

"Got it!" Kevin barely took his eyes off the trail to glance at Jake.

Beth couldn't take her eyes off Jake to look at the trail.

Jake rejoined Beth at the front of the wagon train. He motioned for her to drop back so Kevin could actually lead the way.

The gesture wasn't lost on Kevin. He looked back occasionally, making sure that everyone was following him. He was the cutest kid.

Jake really liked Kevin. Beth had done an excellent job in raising him. If he were ever fortunate enough to have children of his own someday, he'd consider himself lucky if they were at all like Kev.

He couldn't stop stealing glances at Beth. He didn't know what to say to her. Last night had been the best night of his life, and he hoped she felt the same.

Not only was she a giving lover, but he had felt things that he'd never felt with another woman. But that didn't change their situation.

He'd have to find some private time to talk to her about last night. He had to make it clear to her that he wasn't the settling-down type.

Whatever there was between them had to end when her stay at the Gold Buckle Ranch did.

Chapter Eleven

After seeing that all the kids had their breakfast, Jake and Beth took their plates and coffee and sat by the bank of the Silver River.

After last night, there were many things that Jake wanted to say to Beth, but he didn't know where to start. Before she figured on roping and hog-tying him, he wanted to make it clear that there was nothing more between them than sex.

But that would be a lie. And Jake Dixon might be a lot of things, but a liar wasn't one of them.

He loved her.

There. He had finally admitted it. When he delivered Thunder with his four white socks and he saw how her face lit up, he fell in love with her.

But what was the sense? They'd go their separate

ways after Wheelchair Rodeo was over. That's the way it should be.

Nothing he'd ever do would convince her that he wasn't a drinker. And even a woman as interesting and caring as Beth couldn't keep him from riding bulls.

For now, he'd be content just looking at her, watching her every move, committing her to memory.

"Wyoming is a beautiful state," Beth said, taking a sip of coffee. "All of the Gold Buckle Ranch is just magnificent."

"The ranch sits on the prettiest part of Wyoming, but then again, I'm prejudiced."

"Look there!" Beth pointed to an eagle soaring on the breeze.

"A golden eagle," Jake said. "I never get tired of seeing them. How's Cookie's breakfast?"

She dragged a piece of bacon through the yolk of her egg. "Still greasy, but I think I'm getting used to it."

They ate their meal in comfortable silence, looking at the scenery and listening to the gentle flow of the river.

Jake cleared his throat, figuring that he might as well say what was on his mind. "Sorry I had to leave in such a hurry this morning. I wanted to stay longer."

"I wanted you to stay too."

Jake reached for her hand and held it in his. "I thought you'd have regrets."

"No regrets." She traced the back of his hand with a finger. "We reached out for each other. We made love, and it was beautiful. Soon, you go back to bull riding, and I go back home."

His heart sank. This was supposed to be *his* speech!

Beth's gaze remained on the eagle.

This wasn't how the scene was supposed to unfold. He wanted her arms around his neck, her body pressed against his, and sweet, sweet words of everlasting love.

"Well, what do we do now?" he asked.

Beth glanced at him quickly, then looked away again. "I don't know. I didn't know there was a decision to make."

"We'll just steal time to sneak away and have sex until I have to drive you and Kevin to the airport." He raised an eyebrow. "Is that what you want?"

"I didn't say that." She let out a deep breath, looked at him, then looked back at the river. "Is that what *you* want?"

"I didn't say that, either."

He didn't know what he wanted. She was right. She'd be going back to her life in Arizona and he'd be going back on the road. That's what he did.

She smiled weakly. "I think we need to get back to work right now. I have to check on Kathy and Marylou."

"I asked my mother to keep an eye on your girls." He checked his watch. "We have some time yet before we have to move on." He was handling the whole discussion badly, but he didn't want her to go just yet. "Tell me about Lizard Rock."

"There isn't much to tell." She shrugged. "I have a job I pretty much hate, but I keep it because they have an indoor pool for Kevin to do his water therapy, and my time is pretty flexible for the most part. Inez, the owner, is an old friend of my mother's. Actually, she's come to be more my friend than my mother's."

Jake drank his coffee. "That's the first time I've heard you talk about your mother. Is she still alive?"

"She's alive and well in Boca Raton, Florida. She's on her fourth husband, and my father is on his third wife. I think they are having a competition as to who can marry the most."

"They're not involved in your life? Don't they see Kevin?"

"They remember us on Christmas. I get a Christmas card with some money in it from each of them, and so does Kevin. I send them both a Christmas card in return, and Kevin and I enclose a letter. That's about the extent of our relationship with my parents. Brad's parents both died when he was young, so there are no grandparents on that side for Kevin, either."

"Your folks never call?"

"No."

Jake shook his head. How could parents forget that they have a daughter and a grandson? "Did they help out after the accident?"

"Mom was getting married to number three at the time and couldn't get away. Dad was in Europe with number two. They both married well. After the accident, they each called me about once a week to check on Kevin, and they sent me some money for his medical expenses, but that was it." She took a ragged breath. Her fists tightened. "They never came to Brad's funeral. They never came to visit Kevin."

Tears welled in her eyes, and Jake pulled her close to him, allowing her soft curves to mold against him. "I just don't get it."

"I think I stayed with Brad as long as I did because I didn't want my marriage to fail." Her head dropped against the hollow of his shoulder. "Over the years I've come to realize that it wasn't me. My parents are just self-centered."

She straightened, but didn't move away from him. Her eyes had taken on a surprised look, as if the fact that she'd talked so frankly about her personal pain was startling. Unexpected. For a moment, Jake was afraid she'd stop. That she'd pull away and shut down. But she didn't.

"I think that it was a complete surprise when my mother got pregnant with me. They didn't know how to handle a baby. They tried, and for a little while, we lived in the suburbs and superficially things were okay. But they both were restless. After they finally divorced, I was bounced from one to the other."

She pulled up a little yellow flower and inhaled its fragrance. "But you know what bothers me most?"

He saw the hurt in her green eyes. "What's that?"

"They don't seem to care about their only grandchild."

He shook his head. "I can't understand people like that. It's their loss, though. Kevin is one likable young man. You've done a good job raising him."

"Thank you." The hurt in her eyes receded. "Your parents didn't do so bad with you, either. You're a pretty nice guy."

He grimaced. "Only pretty nice?"

"Wonderfully nice. Fabulously nice."

"That's the best you can do?"

"Yes!" She laughed and was back to her old self. "Speaking of your parents, they have such a loving relationship. They're so warm and happy, and look what they do for the kids."

"They are pretty special."

"What was it like growing up with them?"

"We had horses and cattle and wide-open spaces. What more could a kid want? All of us kids were assigned chores. When they were done, the day was our own. We'd swim in the river here. Hunt for treasure. Ride our horses. We'd catch snakes and let them loose in the bunkhouse. Then we'd peek through the windows and watch the ranch hands go crazy. Every day was an adventure."

She chuckled. "And you were loved." She stared off in the distance.

"A day never went by when we weren't hugged or kissed by one or both of them. They went to all of our games. They watched me rodeo as much as they could. They went to all of Ty's science fairs and all of Cody's band concerts. And Karen's plays."

"Your mother told me that they're all in college now." This time she plucked a purple flower and studied it. "I envy you. You grew up with siblings, had lots of friends and wonderful parents."

It would be so easy to tell her that he loved her—it was the perfect time—but how could he? He wouldn't be around for Beth or Kevin any more than her parents or her husband had been. She deserved a husband who'd be there for her. Someone who'd be a father to Kevin.

And if he wasn't healthy or got severely injured, he didn't want her to end up with another invalid. She had her hands full with Kevin.

Dammit, he couldn't even make love to her the way he wanted to.

She reached up and touched the side of his face. "You're not thinking, are you, Jake? I thought we agreed that thinking was a dangerous thing."

"Maybe you and Kev could come to some of my bull-riding events."

"All of my money will be going for Kevin to see specialists in Boston. I need to find out what else can be done for him."

"I'll give you the money for Kev's doctors, and I'll send you the money to come to the events."

She took his hand in hers. "That's very generous of you, but I don't want to take your money. You're going to need it yourself. Let's face it, you're probably going to have to have surgery soon."

"Money isn't a problem for me. And I might even have one sponsor left who hasn't dumped me yet—Wyoming Wear. I'm going to do some modeling for them for some magazine and newspaper ads and do some posing for their catalog." He wiggled his eyebrows. "Ain't that a hoot?"

"I can see you modeling. You're very handsome in a rugged, cowboy way."

His hand flew to his heart and he patted it. "Oh, baby!"

"Oh no. Me and my big mouth. I've created a monster." She giggled.

He loved it when she laughed, but it didn't last long.

"You are going to have an operation if it's called for, aren't you?" she asked.

He shook his head. "I have to get back on the tour."

She stood and held up her hands in defeat. "Did a bull stomp on your brain? What if you get a permanent injury?"

"It won't happen."

"Are you sure of that?"

"Sure enough."

He struggled to get up. He wasn't getting any better, and the little bit of horseback riding he did was killing him.

Her hands on her hips, she squinted at him. "Should I go and get a horse so you can rope the saddle horn and let it pull you to your feet again?"

"Just get a couple of cowboys who aren't busy."

Beth raised her eyes to the sky. Must be another eagle that she wanted to watch.

The wagon train poked along the bank of the river. Kevin was still at the helm. Clint Scully strummed his guitar. In another wagon, someone was telling stories.

After forty-five minutes, they reached the campground at the bend of the river, probably just a couple of miles from where they had eaten breakfast.

Three wooden buildings, all marked with signs, bordered the back of a large grassy clearing. The signs read Girls' Outhouse, Boys' Outhouse and Little Cabin in the Pines. A fourth building, long and low, was a barn with a corral on the side.

"It's my parents' cabin," Jake explained, without being asked. "Mom said that she was too old to stay in a tent, so Dad built the little cabin for her. It doubles as an infirmary and it has a CB radio in it in case of an emergency. Dad calls it their Honeymoon Cabin."

"How romantic," Beth said, looking at the cute cabin with the lace curtains, nestled in the trees that overlooked a grassy carpet of green and a bluer-than-blue mountain lake. "And there's certainly a pretty view." Which would soon be obstructed by the tents for the overnight.

As soon as they dismounted, a cowboy took their horses and led the animals toward the barn. A buzz of activity began as everyone helped in some way to set up camp.

Jake and Kevin worked together putting up the tents. Kevin watched Jake with complete adoration, hanging on to his every word and doing his best to help.

Beth wondered if Jake realized just how much Kevin idolized him. So far, Jake had turned out to be the perfect role model for Kevin, just as Beth had hoped.

There were no more drinking incidents, but then, Jake's own policy forbid any alcohol when they were on duty with the kids.

Beth helped unload the wagons and distribute the mountain of overnight bags into the hands of the rightful owners. She made sure everyone got a sleeping bag. Then it was her job to get the girls settled into their tents.

They were giggly with excitement. For most, it was their first camping experience. They couldn't take their eyes off the boys, and when they found out that Beth was Kevin's mother, she fielded dozens of questions.

"He's so cute. Does he have a girlfriend?"

"What's his e-mail addy?"

"Why is he in a wheelchair?"

"Do you live around here?"

"Does he play any sports?"

She hated to tell them that Kevin's head was turned not by pretty girls, but by horses, cowboys and a rope endorsed by Jake Dixon.

While they were ogling her son, she was ogling Jake Dixon. Right now he was bent over, pounding a tent stake into the ground. She could sense him, no matter where he was, no matter what he was doing. Sometimes she caught him looking at her, and they'd smile. Other times, he'd catch her looking at him. It was so high school, and she loved every minute of it.

The softball game was always the highlight of the campout for Jake. No one could be funnier than Clint Scully as pitcher. They used a beach ball, and the bat was a big orange plastic monstrosity that Clint had found in a clown catalog.

The kids wheeled around the bases, and no matter what happened, Clint and the cowboys always saw to it that the game always ended with the kids winning by one run when Cookie rang the bell for lunch.

Jake was the umpire and his calls were always controversial. He and Clint played off one another to the delight of the kids and the spectators. Cowboys dropped balls and tripped and fell as the kids circled the bases. Hysterical laughter rang out across the peaceful valley.

That was the best medicine, as far as Jake was concerned.

But when the lunch bell rang, he was grateful. Finally, he could take the weight off his leg. He looked for Beth, but Trot called him over to his picnic table.

"Could that cheeseburger be any bigger?" Jake asked, sitting down with a thankful sigh.

"It's Cookie's Ramrod Special. It's about three pounds of raw meat cooked enough to hold it together.

Then he tops it with a pound of raw onions, a brick of cheese and a bottle of ketchup. He puts it between two loaves of Italian bread and hands it to you on a flimsy paper plate."

"The infirmary is going to be crowded after this meal," Jake quipped.

Trot suddenly became serious. "The hospital called me with the results of your X rays. You want the good news or the bad news first?"

"Give me the good news."

"Let's talk leg first. Your tib-fib fracture isn't healing right. You have a non-union going, but it can be fixed. You'll also be able to tell the weather with it from then on. There's going to be a lot of rehab, but it'll be okay."

"And the bad?"

"It's your back. You have a compression fracture of the lumbar spine. I'm worried about more injury to your back if you keep riding. I could give you the medical jargon, but to make it short, your back's a mess. It can be fixed with a fusion and a plug from your hip, but you won't have the flexibility you once had."

Trot's eyes locked with Jake's, and Jake knew what his friend was going to say. He held his breath. *Please don't say it.*

"Partner, my advice to you would be to retire from bull riding. It's too risky."

Damn. "Even after the operations?"

"Yes. Too risky."

"What if I don't have the operations, Trot?"

"You'll be in constant pain with your back, and paralysis is always a possibility, though numbness would precede the paralysis. You'll continue to limp like you do now, and the pain will increase because you're throwing off your posture—that's going to hurt your back even more."

"But you can fix me up? And I could ride again, although it would be risky?"

"I'm good," Trot said, shaking his head, "but I don't want my good work wasted. Think about it, Jake. If you want to talk further, you know where to find me."

"Right here. It's going to take you a week to eat the Ramrod Special."

Trot nodded and took a big bite out of the burger. "Now get lost and go eat with someone prettier than me, like that little gal over there that can't keep her eyes off you. Or maybe it's me she's looking at."

"Not every woman is after you, Trot."

"What do you mean? I was just named 'Catch of the Year' by *Rodeo Wrangler Magazine.*" He took a long draw on a can of root beer.

"She's Kevin's mother, Beth Conroy."

"I know. I'd like to talk to her, too."

"Can I ask why?"

"About Kevin."

Jake felt a hot rush of panic shoot through his chest. "Kevin's okay, isn't he, Trot? Tell me that the kid's okay."

Trot put his monster of a sandwich down and blotted his hands and mouth with a paper napkin. "That's what has me crazy. Kevin seems perfectly okay. I examined him and read his folder from cover to cover. I even called the surgeon who did his last operation. There is no reason why Kevin isn't up and out of that wheelchair and running around Wyoming."

"Damn." Jake thought for a moment. "There must be something that you all overlooked. In case you haven't noticed, the kid is still on wheels."

"I don't get it, either. My guess is that it's something psychological. Maybe I'll call my pal Jesse Goodwin. He's a child psychologist. I'll see if he wants to come up for a Ramrod Special in exchange for a little one-on-one with Kevin. Okay with you?"

"If it's okay with Beth." Jake stood up slowly, feeling every ache and pain. He clamped a hand on Trot's shoulder. "Thanks."

"Don't mention it. We'll talk more."

Trot's concentration returned to his lunch.

Jake suddenly lost his appetite.

After lunch, there were a couple hours of rest and relaxation. Trot and staff passed out meds. Some of the kids actually nodded off in their tents. Some listened to their headphones, some read, most of them talked and joked in groups.

Jake lay along the bank of the river, his hat over his eyes, the sweet, warm breeze drifting over him. The rush of the water calmed him, lulled him into a state of tranquility.

He sensed when Beth approached. He could smell her scent—a scent that was uniquely her own, a mix of sunshine and musky roses.

She sat down next to him but didn't speak, seeming content to just be at this pretty spot. He might have dozed off—he didn't know—but when he woke up, she was still there, staring at the glistening river.

"Hi. Have a nice nap?" she said quietly.

"Hmm…how long was I out?"

"An hour or so."

"I'd better get moving. It's swim time and all volunteers are needed."

"That means me, too," she added.

He stretched, trying to wake up his muscles along with his brain.

"Jake, I saw you talking with Dr. Trotter. Did he have any news about your X rays?" Her eyes showed concern.

Jake didn't want to talk about it, didn't even want to think about giving up his career. Besides, he had a bounty bull to ride for Wheelchair Rodeo.

"Trot and I were talking about Kevin." It was half the truth.

Her eyes grew wide in alarm.

"No. No. Nothing's wrong. Like you, he can't understand why Kevin isn't walking. He has a friend who's a child psychologist. He was going to ask him to talk to Kevin, but only if that's okay with you."

Her face lit up. "I was thinking of something like that myself, but…well…"

"Don't worry about the cost. Trot feels he can lure this special shrink here in exchange for Cookie's cooking."

"Thank you," she whispered, then her voice gained strength. "But I can pay for it. I can pay in installments depending on the cost, and—"

"Whoa! It's part of the program. I've been thinking that we need a psychologist on staff from now on." Actually, he had never thought of it, but it did seem like a good idea for both kids and caretakers alike. "So it'll be free of charge."

"No. I couldn't."

He took a deep breath. "Can't you just let someone help you?"

She stared at him as if he were speaking a foreign language. "I've always done everything by myself."

"Well, now this is one thing you don't have to do by yourself. Can you handle that?"

"I'll try," she said, a twinkle in her eye. "Funny, I remember calling you an amateur cowboy-psychologist once."

"I remember. It was when I told you to give Kevin some space." He tried to get up but his leg was numb. Boy, this was getting old. He was a pitiful wreck. "You listened to me. You gave him some space."

"And Kevin's doing fine. He's made a lot of new friends, and he has an autograph book full of signatures. He has gone through five disposable cameras and has enough memories for a lifetime."

"And what about his mother?"

"I didn't collect any autographs, and I didn't take any pictures, but I'll enjoy Kevin's. I've met several people that I'll keep in contact with when I get back home." She met his eyes. "And I have memories that I'll never forget."

He took her hand and gave it a squeeze.

Emily and Dex Dixon were trying to talk Kevin into finishing the fourth grade before he quit to work at the Gold Buckle Ranch.

"There's a lot to running a ranch, Kevin. It's hard work, and you have to have a lot of smarts up here—" Dex Dixon pointed to his temple. "We use computers now to keep records of the cattle and horses. When it's breeding time, we keep track of—ugh!"

Emily jabbed him in the ribs with her elbow before he mentioned animals being in heat.

"We'd love for you to work for us, Kevin," Em said. "But you need a high school diploma at least. Some of our full-time help even have college degrees."

At the sound of distant laughter, all three turned to see Jake and Beth walking toward them holding hands.

Kevin said the one word that they were all thinking: "Wow!"

Emily tried to be casual, but Dex saw right through her. It wasn't as if Jake held hands with a pretty woman every day—at least, not around them.

"So you just go to college, Kevin," Em said.

Kevin pointed to Jake. "But Jake's the best cowboy in the world, and he didn't go to college. Isn't that right, Jake? And Jake's a zillionaire!"

Jake looked at his father for help. "I think I missed the beginning of this movie."

"Kevin was just telling us that he wants to quit school and work for the Gold Buckle," Dex said. "We were telling him that he needs a college degree."

Jake nodded, getting the drift. "We have high standards at the GBR. After you go to college, we'll talk."

"But that's so far away! And *you* didn't go to college. Your official Web site said that you left for the rodeo trail after high school. That's really cool. You are the coolest."

"My brother is cooler. He's going to be a veterinarian—an animal doctor. He knows a lot about ranching, too. My other brother Cody is way cooler than I am, too. He plays a mean guitar and goes to college in Texas. My sister is at UNLV right now."

He dropped Beth's hand to push Kevin's wheelchair.

"Cool is learning everything you can. I've always regretted not going to college."

"Really?" Kevin looked up at him wide-eyed, soaking up every word he said.

"Really."

"What did you want to be, Jake?"

"I wanted to be just what I am, but if I'd gone to college, I would have studied history. I enjoy reading and learning about all the people who made this country great."

"But *you're* great, Jake. You're in the Cowboy Hall of Fame and the Rodeo Hall of Fame. I read about you all the time. You made history."

Jake stopped dead in his tracks. It was as if a lightning bolt had hit him. He *had* made history, at least in the rodeo world. He was with the best when he was inducted. Bull riders like Donnie Gay, Lane Frost and Tuff Hedeman… All-around cowboys like Larry Mahan, Jim Shoulders and Ty Murray…

He'd never thought about it before, but yeah, he'd made history.

He'd broken long-standing records of cowboys he'd idolized as a child. He'd worked long and hard, learned his craft, studied tapes of rides and picked the brains of the best. He'd spent endless hours on the road traveling from event to event. He'd made his mark.

He was the best once. He wanted to be the best again. He wanted to win the Finals in Vegas.

"It's true, dear," his mother said. "You have made history."

"We've always been proud of you, son, college or not," Dex added.

Beth squeezed his hand. "I think you should go down in the history books, not only for your bull-riding wins or because you held the record for the most ninety-point rides, but because you created Wheelchair Rodeo for kids like Kevin."

"Yeah, Jake," Kevin added. "You're major cool."

A warm feeling settled over him. He was with all the people he loved the most in the world and he didn't have anything more to prove.

So why wasn't that enough for him?

"Thanks. I appreciate it," he mumbled, feeling suddenly uncomfortable. He checked his watch. "We'd better get ready for swim time."

They all walked slowly toward the tent area, content in one another's company.

"What guys in history do you think are cool, Jake?" Kevin asked.

"Hey, don't forget about the women who made history. Ladies like Eleanor Roosevelt, Harriet Tubman, Elizabeth Cady Stanton, Sacagawea."

"But what *guys?*"

"Christopher Columbus, Abe Lincoln, Davy Crockett, Sitting Bull, Babe Ruth, George Custer, Jim Bowie…"

"The rock star?" Kevin asked.

Jake chuckled. "No, that's David Bowie. Jim was at the Alamo."

"Oh."

"Did you learn about the Alamo yet?" Jake asked.

"No."

"See why you have to go to school?"

"Yeah," Kevin conceded.

"Good. That's settled." Jake rubbed his hands together. "Now, let's get changed and go swimming."

"Cool."

Jake thought that there were several times in life that really deserved to be classified as magnificent, and this was definitely one of those times.

Last night with Beth was another.

Chapter Twelve

The sun was bright and high in the sky. Only a slight breeze bent the long grass on the bank of the river.

Excitement charged the air as the kids got ready to swim. They were slathered with sunscreen, belted into life jackets and assigned to groups. There were about three adults to each swimmer. One was a medical person, one was a volunteer and the third was a certified Red Cross lifeguard. Extra medical staff were all on high alert.

Beth was assigned to a young girl named Eileen who was both thrilled to be going swimming for the first time in a "real outdoor place" and scared silly. Dr. Trotter was also on her team, along with a perky California-type blond lifeguard named Cheryl "Call me Cher" O'Brien.

Cher cut an attractive figure in her red one-piece

bathing suit. Beth felt like her tropical two-piece with a skirt looked like a reject from a muumuu factory. She didn't have a speck of tan, and after seeing Cher and a couple of the women, she vowed to lose twenty pounds when she got back home.

Dr. Trotter was patient and encouraged Eileen with jokes and teasing. Soon she was splashing him and letting her legs dangle in the water.

"I've never been swimming outside before!" Eileen giggled as she coughed up some water. "It's cold!"

"Do you want to float on your back?" suggested Cher.

"Will I sink?" Eileen asked.

"Not with that life jacket on and all of us here. Want to try it?"

"Yes!"

Beth stood watch with Dr. Trotter as Cher moved Eileen carefully in the water. Frequently, Cher's eyes drifted to Dr. Trotter, who looked quite studly in his boxer-type bathing suit.

Dr. Trotter pointed to Kevin splashing Jake about thirty yards from them. "Kevin seems to be doing quite well."

"The apartment building that I manage has an indoor pool," Beth explained. "A physical therapist comes and gives Kevin water therapy. He's very comfortable in the water."

"I can see that," the doctor said, never taking his eyes off Eileen. "Did Jake mention the child psychologist that's a pal of mine? He owes me a few favors, and I'd like him to talk to Kevin. Is that okay with you?"

"Jake did mention it. It's fine with me, Dr. Trotter.

There's nothing I won't try to get Kevin out of that wheelchair."

"That's what I thought you'd say."

"Obviously, you think it's something psychological?"

He gave a slight nod. "That's not my area of expertise, but, in my opinion, there's no medical condition keeping Kevin in that chair. It could very well be psychological."

"Knowing Kevin, if he could, he'd be running all over this ranch. I can't imagine what would keep him sitting in that chair if it wasn't physical, but I'd love for your friend to talk to him."

"Good." He looked at Cher. "Would you like me to take over now?"

"Okay." Cher flashed brilliant white teeth and perky breasts as she bent over.

After a while, Dr. Trotter decided that Eileen was tiring and needed to sit in shallow water or lie down on a blanket on shore.

Eileen didn't want to stop. "I feel so light!" she said. "It's so good not to be sitting."

"After you rest, you can swim again," he promised.

Eileen chose to lie down on the blanket and not sit in her chair, so the doctor and another cowboy carried her to the blanket, where she joined a hot game of Old Maid.

There was nothing for Beth to do just yet, so she sat on a chair. Her position gave her a good view of Jake and Kevin. They were playing some kind of volleyball, and looked like they were having the time of their lives.

Why couldn't Brad have paid more attention to his

son? She knew the answer to that. His job and his drinking were more important.

Kevin had adored his father and had been grateful for any kind of attention from him. It had always broken her heart to see Kevin so wanting for his father to notice him. She had brought it up to Brad many times, and for a while he had improved, but when his drinking increased, his interest in his family decreased.

Doc Trotter pulled up a chair next to her. "Those two are inseparable, aren't they."

"Kevin idolizes Jake. Jake has been his hero when he needed one. It's done him a world of good to actually meet Jake and be with him."

"Kevin's done a world of good for Jake, too. So have you."

"I don't know about that."

"I do. You and Kevin are all he talks about."

Beth raised an eyebrow and gave a little grunt.

The doctor laughed. "Well, other than riding bulls."

"That's more like it."

"He has some hard decisions to make. He's going to need some friends."

Beth felt a lump rise to her throat. "What do you mean?"

"He'll have to tell you the rest. But I know you went with him to the hospital when he had X rays, and you have some idea as to his injuries." Dr. Trotter winked. "So maybe you can find a way to pry things out of him and help him. He's tight-lipped about things that concern him."

"You got the results of the X rays, didn't you."

"Yes."

"And?"

"And that's why I said that he has some tough decisions to make." He stood up. "I've already said too much." His eyes sparkled. "Darn that doctor-patient confidentiality."

Dinner was what Cookie called his Chuck Wagon Extravaganza. It was basically Sloppy Joes heaped on a roll, a mountain of french fries and corn on the cob.

"Mom, the food is so good here," Kevin said. "I'm going to miss Cookie's cooking. Do you think he could give you some pointers?"

Jake unsuccessfully tried to hide the laughter bubbling up inside him. Kevin's sideways glance at Jake gave it away that they were in cahoots.

She watched them high-five one another. They got along so perfectly.

"I think you're absolutely right, Kevin. Why, Cookie was just telling me how he makes a rattlesnake burger that's just delicious. He says it tastes just like chicken. He's going to give me the recipe."

Kevin put his hands on his throat as the smile left his face. "You're kidding, aren't you?"

Jake nudged him. "You're not falling for that, are you?"

"Uh…no! No. No way would I fall for a lame thing like that. Rattlesnake burger! No way."

It was Beth's turn to laugh.

She touched Kevin's cheek with the palm of her hand. When she glanced up at Jake, their gazes locked. She loved her son, but her heart ached for Jake Dixon.

The ache was so deep and unfamiliar that it humbled her with its intensity.

She didn't want him to hurt anymore. She wanted him safe and free of pain. But how was that possible? He had picked one of the most dangerous jobs in the world—one that served him up an adrenaline rush but trashed his body on a regular basis. If he kept riding bulls, he was bound to get hurt again. Maybe next time it would be permanent.

Beth didn't think she could stand to see that happen—not even for a million-dollar ride for Wheelchair Rodeo. Darn that Harvey Trumble for putting strings on his donation.

She wanted to talk to Jake about what Dr. Trotter had told him, but not in front of Kevin.

She didn't have to wait long. One of the boys from his tent motioned him over, and Kevin hurried away. Jake sat down next to her.

"The joke about Cookie teaching you how to cook was Kevin's idea," Jake said.

She chuckled. "Why do I think you were the instigator?" Her lips formed into a tight, stern line. "Jake?"

"Uh-oh. You've got that serious look. What's up?"

"Tell me about your conversation with Dr. Trotter."

He froze for a minute with a forkful of Sloppy Joe en route to his mouth. "Let's not talk about it now. I have to think about what he said."

"So it's not good news?"

He shook his head. "Let's just have fun right now, Beth. It's nothing that can't wait."

"But I'm concerned about you."

He put his fork down. "I appreciate that, but don't

worry about me. You just have a good time on the camp-out."

Beth's heart sank. "After what we've shared, I thought you'd at least open up to me about this."

He took a deep breath. "Talking about myself is not that easy for me. I need time. I just don't want to talk about it yet, not to you, not to anyone. It's something I have to think about."

She picked up her tray. "Okay. That's your prerogative. I shouldn't have butted into your business. But as someone said to me recently, 'Can't you just accept help?'"

Jake reached up and touched her arm. "This is different," he said.

"How?"

"It just is."

She shook her head. "Jake, look at what you do for the kids and their families. Everyone here would jump off a bridge if you asked them to. Anyone here would lend you an ear if you needed one." She gently pulled free. "And that goes double for me.

"I don't want to be your mother. I already have a son." It took all of her strength to get up. "You know where to find me if you decide you want to talk."

She took her tray and sat by Kathy and Marylou. She half listened to their chatter, but her gaze kept drifting back to Jake. It didn't take him long to get back to his clipboard and walk away.

She didn't feel much like eating. She wanted to be back at the Trail Boss Cabin where she could immerse herself in a good book and forget about strong, silent cowboys.

She took her two charges to the rest room. Later she watched as they primped in front of the mirrors.

"I'm going to sit next to Clint Scully at the campfire," Marylou announced. "He's so hot!"

Kathy ran a brush through her hair. "I'm going to sit next to T.J. He's cuter than anyone here." She turned toward Beth. "Mrs. Conroy, aren't you going to put any makeup on?"

"Can I fix your hair, Mrs. Conroy?" Marylou asked, holding up a clear plastic purse filled with cosmetics.

Beth looked at herself in the mirror. Her hair was a fright from swimming. Her face showed every blemish in the harsh fluorescent lights.

"Okay, ladies. Go for it."

"Sit down on the bench over there, so we can reach you."

For the next twenty minutes, Beth was painted, blotted, sprayed and fussed over. When they finally let her look at the finished project, she had to admit that the girls had talent. She looked good!

"Is that me?" Beth asked in amazement.

"That's you. You look beautiful! I'll bet Jake Dixon will fall over in his boots."

"Jake?" Beth asked. Was it that obvious?

"He's got eyes for you, Mrs. Conroy. He's always watching you and drooling."

"Kevin wants you to marry him. Are you going to marry him, Mrs. Conroy?"

"Hey, hang on a minute!" She tried to catch her breath. What on earth was Kevin telling everyone? "I think you're putting the cart before the horse."

"Huh?"

"I think we'd better get to the campfire, so you ladies can join in. Okay?"

"Yeah."

"And thanks for the help."

"Oh, wait. One more thing," Kathy said. "Close your eyes."

She did as instructed, expecting a hit of perfume. Instead, she felt a brush on her cheeks.

"What's that?" Beth asked.

"Glitter."

"Glitter? As in the stuff that…glitters?"

"Fairy green. It'll be really sparkly in the campfire light."

"Oh." She couldn't appear in public with green glitter on her face, but she didn't have the heart to wash their efforts off her face. "Thanks, ladies."

"You're welcome."

"Shall we go back to the tent and get your jackets? It'll be cool later. Maybe you should put on some sweatpants, too."

They nodded and then talked about what they should wear and what jewelry they should put on.

Beth tried to remember if she was ever that young.

As she approached the campfire, one of the cowboys handed her a stick and a bag of marshmallows.

Kevin's jaw dropped when he saw her. "Mom, what did you do to your face?"

"Why, what do you mean?"

"You're all sparkly, like…uh…"

"Glitter," Jake supplied, taking the bag of marshmallows from her and putting one on the end of her stick. "Just like new-fallen snow."

"It's green." She chuckled. "Kathy and Marylou gave me a makeover."

Kevin scrunched up his nose. "Like, why?"

"Oh, no reason."

"You look better without that green stuff."

"You look beautiful," Jake whispered in her ear.

She shivered from his warm breath on her cool skin.

"Here, sit down." He motioned to a bench, then sat down beside her.

She passed her stick with the marshmallow to Kevin. "Never did like them."

"Hello, everyone." Emily and Dex moved into the circle.

There were greetings all around. Then Kevin turned his concentration to firing up his marshmallow.

Emily leaned over and said quietly, "Jake, I was just thinking that you should show Beth the hot spring. It's beautiful at night. Ghostly. The steam rises and..." She looked up at Dex and smiled.

Beth could see the happiness on her face, the glow. It was then that she noticed Emily's and Dex's hair was damp. It must be a romantic hot spring.

Jake was just about to object, when Dex handed him a flashlight. "Son, there's nothing going on that we can't keep an eye on. Go now, and show Beth the hot spring. Maybe take a little dip. I'll bet it's something that she's never seen. Besides, it'll be good for your leg and back."

Beth felt a nervous excitement when Jake stood and held his hand out to her.

"I should have thought of it myself. Thanks, Mom... Dad."

"Take your time," Emily replied. "We'll keep an eye on Kevin."

Beth glanced at her son. He was busy with his friends torching marshmallows. Clint was about to begin a story. Kevin would indeed be fine.

Jake and Beth walked away from the glow of the campfire and the floodlights, past the corral of horses. Their path behind the infirmary through the pines was lit only by the full moon.

"We don't bring the kids to the hot spring because it's a tough path. The wheelchairs wouldn't make it. It's a well-kept secret. Only a few people know about it."

They continued to walk as Jake guided her down a narrow clearing. The laughter of the camp faded as they walked. Other than the faint hoot of an owl, it was a quiet night.

A while later, she found herself in a clearing. A stream gurgled swiftly, then disappeared into a circle of water that sparkled in the moonlight. Rocks and boulders surrounded the shimmering pool. Steam dissipated as it rose higher, coating the leaves and needles of the surrounding trees with shiny moisture.

"Oh, Jake! I've never seen such a place!"

"It's my favorite spot on the ranch. You should see it in winter. The trees are frosted with ice and snow. It looks like a Christmas card."

"It's so...ethereal." Beth took a deep breath. "I want to go in but I didn't bring a bathing suit."

"Funny thing, neither did I." His eyes sparked with

mischief. "I guess we'll have to go back to the campfire and listen to Clint's ghost stories."

He turned to leave.

"Okay." Two could play his game. "You go ahead. I'll catch up. I think I'll stay and take a dip. Alone."

He looked over his shoulder.

"Or you could join me," she finished.

His sexy smile made her heart leap. Without breaking eye contact, he hooked his hat on the branch of a tree as naturally as if he'd done it a hundred times before. She pulled her T-shirt off and draped it over a limb on the same tree. They dispensed with the rest of their clothes in short order and stood looking at each other.

In two steps, Jake had her in his arms, skin against skin, cool from the night breeze.

"I feel like Adam and Eve in the Garden of Eden," Beth said when she found her voice.

His lips came down over hers. She felt the length of him against her. "Mmm…"

The gentle lapping of the water and the haunting hoot of an owl were the only sounds she heard. His hands cupped her breasts as he nibbled her neck. The misty steam enveloped them, caressed them, cocooned them, as if they were the only people in the world.

When she was back in Arizona, she'd never forget this moment, this man.

Jake ran a finger down her nose. "You're beautiful, you know. All naked and misty in the moonlight. And glittering green."

She chuckled. "You don't look so bad yourself, cowboy." She took his hand and tugged it. "Shall we try your outdoor hot tub?"

"Hang on just a second." He pulled his wallet out of a pocket in his pants and took out two condoms. He held them up to her and she smiled. Then he returned the pants to a tree branch.

They walked between two large rocks down a slight incline. At closer range, she could see that the water bubbled. He helped her in. She was pleasantly surprised at the perfect temperature of the water—not too hot, not too cold.

"It's only about three feet deep here, so don't worry."

She immersed herself to the neck, still surprised at the bubbles. They tickled every nook and cranny of her body. It was like swimming in champagne.

"This is really special. Thanks for bringing me."

"Thank my parents." He chuckled and pointed to a flat rock where there were two folded terry-cloth towels. "The little matchmakers."

"Your parents? Matchmakers?"

"Tell me you haven't figured them out yet. They are about as subtle as a Sherman tank."

She reached for him, ran her hands down his strong arms. "You and me? They're trying to fix us up?"

"Yep."

She laughed. "Interesting."

He took her in his arms and kissed her. His tongue traced the seam of her lips, and she opened her mouth for him. He pulled her even closer and continued his delicious assault.

She found herself lifted off her feet and deposited on a rock ledge. Without taking his eyes off her, he tore open a plastic packet and unrolled a condom over his hard length.

His consideration of her touched her heart. Watching him put it on made her hot.

Then his hands were on her knees. "Open for me."

She did.

Standing between her legs, she felt him enter her, slowly at first; then he buried his length inside her.

He lifted her and she wrapped her legs around him. Their eyes met and she studied his face, memorizing each laugh line, every scar, the curve of his jaw. She brushed back the wet hair from his forehead and kissed him there.

Their lovemaking was unhurried and slow, each knowing it might be the last time they'd be alone. Three days. That's all she had left at the Gold Buckle Ranch. Tomorrow was Wheelchair Rodeo. Saturday was the big Gold Buckle Challenge, and Jake would be busy all day. She and Kevin would be leaving on Sunday.

She pushed that to the back of her mind. She clung to Jake and kissed him with all the passion built up inside her. He buried himself even deeper inside her. Their sighs melded together.

Beth was the first to move, slowly at first, then riding him in a wild frenzy. Their tongues danced, teeth nipped, until Jake shuddered and breathed her name. Her release followed, her sigh of pleasure lost in the warmth of his mouth.

With the mist around them and the canopy of stars sparkling in the night sky, they embraced, not wanting to let go. Not wanting to leave this special place. Not knowing if they'd be able to be alone again before they had to go their separate ways.

Chapter Thirteen

The wagon train slowly returned to the ranch. Kevin led the way again, but this time, he shared the honor with his friends, Alex and Luke.

Jake couldn't think of anything but Beth. The way she rode next to him was as if she'd grown up on the back of a horse. She was a natural. And the way she had looked last night in the hot spring, all bathed in the moonlight and mist…

He'd never forget her. They'd made love with such sweetness, then a second time with wild abandon. Then they had frolicked in the bubbles like two school kids.

What the hell was he doing?

He should be throwing himself into getting the Wheelchair Rodeo competition ready for this afternoon and checking on several other details for the Challenge.

He had a staff of organizers whom he trusted, but many minor things fell to him.

Yet he could only think about finding time to be with Beth.

His gaze shifted to Kevin. If there was another boy who enjoyed being a cowboy more than Kevin Conroy, Jake wanted to meet him. The kid lived to ride horses and rope, and every second that Kevin's smile got bigger and brighter, his mother's eyes lost that haunted, tired looked that he'd noticed the first day he met her.

In a couple of days, Kevin would be leaving, too. Jake's hands tightened on the reins. Shoot. He hadn't realized it until this moment, but he loved the boy as if Kevin were his own son. His leaving would only deepen the hole in Jake's heart.

But they'd take back with them good memories of the Gold Buckle Ranch. It had been a very successful campout. As luck would have it, the weather had cooperated, and they hadn't had any close encounters of the reptile kind.

He and Beth and Kevin could keep in touch. There was e-mail and the phone. But it wouldn't be the same.

Beth rode quietly beside him. Every now and then her thigh would brush up against his. He wanted to take her hand and hold it, to touch her again. Instead, he tried to seem interested when Kevin pointed to another eagle or a jackrabbit scooting into the brush to get out of the way.

He hadn't counted on falling so hard for Beth.

He didn't have anything to offer her other than a broken-down, has-been bull rider. Sure, he was in the Hall of Fame. Sure he had money. But what was he now? Nothing.

He didn't even have a college education like his brothers and sister soon would.

Beth and Kevin deserved someone who would settle down. Not someone who was looking to reclaim his lost fame. Someone who'd be there for them, not someone who was looking for the first flight out of Mountain Springs in the hope of winning another gold buckle and another title.

She leaned toward him and whispered, "Are you ready to talk about what Dr. Trotter told you yet? Or are you still thinking about it?"

"I don't want to give up my bull riding."

"Is that a probability?"

"Yeah, according to Trot. He said both my leg and back will be okay with a couple of operations. If I don't do the operations, I could have permanent injury if I ride and make it worse."

"Permanent? As in pain? What?"

"As in pain and numbness and possibly…paralysis."

Her face drained of color. "Then there's no decision. You have to give up bull riding."

"It's not as simple as that."

"It sure is. Merciful heavens, Jake, do you want to end up in a wheelchair for the rest of your life?"

"Not particularly."

"Then what's the problem?"

"I want to retire on top. I have to stay on the tour to qualify for Vegas in October. I want to win Vegas. But first, I have to ride Twister. Then I'm going to ride in my own event. After I do all that, then maybe I'll retire."

"But you've won everything there is to win. You even won Vegas before."

"It's just something I have to do for myself."

"You'd risk your health for that? And you insist on riding a difficult bounty bull that thirty-five others haven't been able to ride?"

"The bounty bull's for Wheelchair Rodeo." He didn't hesitate. "Yes. I would. That's what I do. That's who I am."

"Bull riding might be what you do, but it's not who you are. You're a hero to these kids—kids who'd never experience any of this if it weren't for you. You have fabulous organizational skills. You put on bull-riding events. You know how to talk to kids without talking down to them. There's nothing you couldn't do, Jake. And if you want to study history, you could do that, too."

"Thanks," he said.

"But?"

"But it's not enough."

Her cheeks flushed red. "You are such a hardheaded, stubborn old mule of a cowboy. You just don't get it."

He shrugged. "Maybe you don't understand how it is."

"Obviously I don't," she snapped.

The Gold Buckle came into view. While they had been gone, several tents had been erected for Wheelchair Rodeo, and more bleachers added near the corral. An excited buzz went through the wagon train.

"Listen to the kids, Jake. Don't you get as much satisfaction when you hear them as you do from an arena full of bull-riding fans?"

He looked toward the ranch and the glittering river, and then back at the kids as they bubbled with enthusiasm and pointed out the tents and the bleachers.

"You know, I like them both, but I got to admit that I get more satisfaction from the kids."

"The prosecution rests."

"I'm still going to ride."

"You might get hurt."

"It's part of the job."

She did a slow burn the rest of the way, trying to figure out how the same man who brought her to ecstasy last night could make her want to rage at him today.

The cowboys and the volunteers unloaded the kids from the horses and the wagons and sent them to the mess hall for lunch. Later, the kids would rest for a while, if they possibly could, and then get ready for Wheelchair Rodeo.

The cowboys would take care of brushing, feeding and watering the horses for today.

Kevin looked back at his horse as if he couldn't bear to part from a lifelong friend. "After lunch, I'll bring you some apples, boy."

Beth walked alongside him as he wheeled to the mess hall. "That'll be after rest time, Kev."

"I don't want to rest. That's for babies."

"You want to be in top shape for the rodeo, don't you?"

"Yeah."

"Then you need to rest."

"Oh, all right," he said grudgingly.

Lunch was tacos and a salad bar. A chicken barbecue and corn roast would come later, after Wheelchair

Rodeo. Thanks to Cookie, they certainly had been eating heartily on this trip. At this rate, she was never going to be able to snap her jeans.

They made a couple of tacos and picked a table by the window to watch the action.

"Jake is the greatest, isn't he, Mom?"

Not again, she thought. She took a deep breath. "He's very nice. Really nice."

"Are you going to marry him?"

When Kevin looked up at her with his big hopeful eyes, it was hard to pick the right words. "Didn't we talk about this before, sweetie? Even though I think he's cool, and I think he thinks I'm cool, we are pretty different. He lives here. We live in Arizona."

"We could move. Don't you like it here?"

His voice was thin as if he might cry. He never cried. He hadn't cried about any of his surgeries.

She put her arm around him and kissed his forehead. "Please, Kevin, don't make this hard. If we save some money, maybe we can come back next year."

His head dropped. "I really like it here, Mom. I like Jake."

"Jake will be bull riding. We can watch him on TV. He wouldn't be around the ranch much until next summer anyway."

"We can go with him on tour. We could cheer him on."

"But he's very busy, and I have my job, and—" She took a deep breath and patted his arm. "Kevin, let's talk about this more later."

In the time it took them to eat, thunderclouds moved in over the ranch, blocking the sun. They could hear a rumbling in the distance.

Jake hurried into the mess hall and announced, "Everyone, get where you're going, please. Take shelter. This looks like it's going to be a bad one."

"What about Wheelchair Rodeo?" Kevin asked.

"We might have to postpone it. Either later tonight, or more than likely it'll be tomorrow."

"Aww...jeez!"

Jake walked over to where they were sitting. "Don't worry, Kev. We'll get it in, even if we have to do it inside the Mountain Springs Arena before the bull riding."

"Oh, wow! Really?"

"Really. Say, the boys have a poker game going at the bunkhouse if you want to join in."

"Poker?" Beth asked.

"It's only for macaroni, Mom."

She laughed. "I knew that." She turned to Jake. "Need any help?"

"Nope. Everything's under control. Why don't you get yourself to your cabin and snuggle in, read a book or whatever." He winked, then whispered in her ear, "I'll try to join you as soon as I can."

She started to tingle all over just thinking of them making love in the cozy cabin during a raging storm. She'd make a fire in the fireplace, put on her Wal-Mart nightgown and they'd snuggle under the comforter.

She watched as Kevin grabbed a couple of apples from the salad bar.

"See you, Mom."

"Okay."

Kevin wheeled off in the direction of the barn with Jake at his side.

She hurried to her cabin as the wind picked up. The

sky was almost blue-black. Fat raindrops fell on her before she reached shelter.

Her gear was already on the front porch. She brought it in and deposited it on a chair. She jumped from a loud clap of thunder and was riveted as lightning flashed bright in the room. Thunderstorms seemed so much louder here than they did in Arizona.

She wasn't scared. It was just so powerful. She took a seat by the window to watch it. The rain came down in torrents, and almost as black as night.

Thank goodness the storm hadn't hit during the campout.

Jake turned the corner of the barn and headed for the refrigerator in the tack room. Opening the door, he popped the top of a cold beer. He was done for the day and wanted some peace and quiet to think about everything that he needed to do for tomorrow. He sat down at his desk and took a long draw of the cold liquid.

Did he love Beth enough to give up riding?

She wanted him to. The last thing she needed was another person in a wheelchair. She'd made that clear enough.

It wouldn't come to that.

Jake took another swig. He put his feet up on the desk and leaned back, tuning in to the rain on the roof, looking out the window to the ranch that he'd helped build.

His brothers, Ty and Cody, weren't interested in the Gold Buckle. They were working on their own careers. He didn't know about his sister, Karen. She seemed quite happy in Vegas. When his parents were ready to retire, he'd buy the place from them and buy his siblings out. Until then, he might build his own cabin near the hot spring.

Beth loved the hot spring.

They could spend long, leisurely nights in the spring together—if he quit riding.

He could tell that she liked him. If she didn't, she wouldn't care whether he rode, whether he had surgery.

But did she love him enough to marry him?

He took another sip from his beer. Nice and cold.

Jake heard a noise. As he struggled to get up, beer sloshed on his shirt.

Brushing it off with his hand, he stepped out into the barn. He almost choked on the gulp he had taken, when he saw Kevin Conroy stand up, walk toward a couple of barrels of hay and pick up an apple from the floor in front of them.

Jake blinked. He must be seeing things.

Kevin walked to the horse's stall and held the apple out to the horse. "Here you go, Killer."

Then he walked back to his wheelchair and got another apple from the canvas bag hanging from it. He fed it to the horse. "Good boy, Killer. Good boy. I'll get you a carrot."

Kevin turned and walked to the carrot basket.

Jake couldn't believe his eyes. "Kevin?"

The boy froze.

"Kevin?" Jake walked closer, squinting. "What the…"

Kevin turned to face Jake. "I—I…uh…"

"How long have you been able to walk?"

He didn't answer. He looked ready to bolt.

"I'm thrilled that you can walk, but how long were you going to fake like that? That's not the cowboy way, son. I'm very disappointed in you."

The boy stared up at him, his eyes tearing up. "That's what my father always said to me. You even smell like him," he blurted.

Jake looked down at the beer can in his hand. He heaved it into a nearby trash can. Shoot. He was handling this whole thing badly.

"Does your mother know you can walk?"

"No." Tears brimmed in his eyes. He blinked, and they trailed down his cheeks, dropping onto his shirt.

Jake held his palms up. "I find that hard to believe. What's this about? A free vacation?" He knew his tone was harsh, but he felt like he was being played for a sucker.

Kevin's whole face crumbled. Jake felt like an ogre, but he couldn't understand why this beautiful boy would sit in a wheelchair when he could walk.

"She doesn't know! I tried to tell her, but I—I..." He reached up to swipe his tears with his shirtsleeve.

Jake felt his stomach knot with dread. He wanted to believe him, he really did.

Maybe it was something psychological, as Doc Trotter thought. If it was, Jake was bungling this. He sure as heck didn't want to make Kevin cry. What kind of an idiot was he?

"Look, I'm not going to tell your mom. I'm going to leave that to you. She'll be happy—not that you lied to her, but because you can walk. I'm happy, too. Now go to the bunkhouse, hang out with the guys and relax. When the storm clears, you can tell your mother."

Kevin nodded and went back to his wheelchair.

"Are you still going to sit in that thing?"

Kevin nodded, his expression a combination of confusion and fear. "I don't want them to know I can walk yet."

Jake shrugged, but he was unable to shake off his disillusionment in Kevin's answer. "I don't get it, but suit yourself."

Kevin started to wheel away, but stopped and looked back. "Jake, can I still be in Wheelchair Rodeo?" His eyes were red rimmed but hopeful. The rest of his face told Jake that he already knew the answer.

"Wheelchair Rodeo is only for kids who can't walk, Kev. You can."

As soon as Kevin's chair disappeared around the corner, Jake stood in the middle of the barn, rehashing how miserably he'd handled things—how he'd do it differently if he had another chance.

"Just goes to show what a lousy father I'd make," he said softly. He picked up a pitchfork and tore into the hay with a vengeance, adding fresh bedding to each stall.

"Anyone see Kevin Conroy?" Jake looked around the bunkhouse.

"He was sitting right here for the longest time," said Ramon.

"Check the bathroom," Jake instructed as he walked out on the porch to look around the area.

The storm showed no signs of letting up. It was still dark out. The rain was falling even faster.

Ramon rushed to his side. "His wheelchair is in

there. A window is open, but there's no sign of Kevin. I'd say he scooted out the window. Is that possible?"

Jake couldn't stand the thought that Kevin was out in the storm. He'd check the barn first. Maybe he was paying Killer another visit, or hiding somewhere.

"Ramon, grab some of the boys and look for him. If you find him, you know the signal."

"If he's on the ranch, we'll find him, boss."

"Thanks."

Jake grabbed his slicker from a hook and hurried out to the barn. Killer was still there, but there was no sign of Kevin. Where would he go?

Jake snapped his fingers. *To talk to his mother.*

Jake ran as fast as he could to Beth's cabin, hoping he'd find Kevin there, safe and sound. He took the stairs two at a time and bit back the screaming pain. He couldn't be bothered with it now. The door of the cabin swung open just as he was about to bang on it.

Beth must have sensed his worry because her smile disappeared.

"I saw you coming. What's wrong?"

"Is Kevin here?" Jake asked.

"No. He's in the bunkhouse."

"No, he's not. He's run away. He ducked out through a window in the bathroom."

"But that's impossible. He can't get up. He can't—"

Jake put his hands on her shoulders and broke the news. "I saw him standing in the barn. I saw him walking."

A look of shock crossed her face. "That's impossible. Jake, why are you saying these things?" She stepped toward him. "You've been drinking! I can smell it. Are you drunk? Is that why you're not making sense?"

"No, I'm not drunk!" He grabbed her elbows and stared into her scared green eyes. "Your son can walk. Believe me."

"Then why…?"

"I don't know." Her eyes told him that she really didn't know that Kevin could walk.

"Maybe he had a good reason—only I never took the time to find out. I was so darn shocked. Look, I have to go. I have to find him."

"If he's out in this storm… Oh, Jake, if anything happens to him!"

"I think I know where he went. Back to the campgrounds. He has to be there. That's the only place I can think of."

She grabbed a coat. "Let's go."

"I can do this faster alone."

"Don't argue with me. He's my son, and you've been drinking. Maybe one of the other cowboys can find him."

He grabbed her arm, stopping her in her tracks. "I am not a drunk! I spilled a can of beer on myself. I was having one drink, one!" He took a long, irritated breath. "Hey, Beth, let's not fight. It's not going to help me find Kevin any faster. I already have some of the boys looking for him." He dropped his arms and turned away. "I was the one who caused him to run away. I'll find him."

Tears fell down her cheeks. "Okay. Hurry."

"When I do, we might stay put for a while, take shelter. Kevin probably needs some dry clothes, and I need to talk to him."

Beth picked up a saddle bag, emptied it, and stuffed some clothes back in. She handed it to Jake. "This'll do. How will I know if you find him?"

"There's a CB radio in my parents' cabin. I'll radio back."

Jake hurried back to the barn to saddle Lance.

When he walked the horse out of the barn, the rain was coming down in sheets. Jake couldn't see two feet in front of him. He knew a shortcut through the woods—that's what he'd take.

If Kevin stuck to the wagon trail and was on foot, Jake would probably beat Kevin to the campgrounds.

Please be there, was Jake's mantra as he led Lance through the pines. He could hear the suction of the horse's hooves on the mud. It was slow going, but only rarely did the horse shy.

Finally Jake could see a shadow against the lights of the cabin through the trees. It had to be Kevin.

"Hey, Kev!" he yelled.

Jake doubted that the kid could hear him over the racket of the storm. He yelled again as loudly as he could. He was just about to dismount when lightning flashed and split a tree.

Lance reared and Jake flew through the air. He landed with a grunt on his back on the wet, muddy ground. Lance galloped off toward the cabin.

Jake tried to catch his breath. Then he coughed up the water that was pouring down on him. He couldn't move, couldn't work up enough strength to sit up. Every bone in his body hurt. The mud beneath him seemed to be sucking him down, rendering him immobile. Figures he'd be in the lowest spot of the entire campgrounds.

"Jake! You okay?" Suddenly Kevin stood above him, yelling over the sound of the storm. At least Kevin had had enough sense to put on a poncho.

"I've felt better. How about you?"

"I'm okay."

"Why did you run off like that, Kev?"

"Because I did everything wrong."

"So? You face it. You don't run away like a little kid. You're a young man now. A cowboy."

"Really?"

"Really." Jake shook off the rainwater that was pouring on his face.

Kevin got Jake's hat out of a nearby puddle and handed it to him.

"Thanks, partner." He held it over his face to keep some of the water off. "Do you think you can help me?"

"You shouldn't move. That's what my health teacher, Mrs. Kazmoski, said."

"I know, but I'm drowning here."

Kevin looked back at the trail. "Do you want me to run back and get Doc Trotter?"

"Hold on. I'll be okay. I just need to get vertical."

"How do I get you up? You're bigger than me."

"Is Lance around? Can you lead him back here?"

"He's by the barn. I can get him, Jake."

"There's a rope on the saddle. Tie one end around the saddle horn. Hand me the other end."

"Okay, Jake. Don't go away."

He chuckled as he wiped the water that was pouring over his face. "I'll be here."

As Jake lay there on his back, it finally sank in that

if a bull ever tossed him, he'd never be able to move out of the way.

Jake thought he heard the sound of a horse coming toward him.

"Kevin! Jake!" He heard Beth shout. She was riding Thunder. He had known she'd never be able to stay put.

She dismounted and rushed to Jake's side. "What happened?"

"Lance got spooked by lightning. I got tossed."

"Are you okay?"

"Hard to say."

"Oh, Jake!" She looked around. "Did you find Kevin?"

Jake knew the exact moment when she saw her son. Her face changed from surprise to disbelief and then pure joy.

"Kevin!" She ran toward him, slipping and sliding in the mud.

"Mom!" He met her halfway. "I can walk! I wanted to tell you."

As the rain fell down on them all, Jake watched Beth hug her son. She was oblivious to the rain and everything else, including him, lying there like a fallen log.

He let Beth enjoy seeing Kevin walk for a minute or two, then he yelled, "Hey, remember me?"

"Mom, Jake fell off the horse and it's all my fault. If I hadn't run away, he'd be okay. All his fans are going to be mad at me if he's hurt. It's all my fault." He sniffed. "I can't do anything right."

"Honey, Jake was hurt long before he landed in this mud, but we'll talk later. Right now, let's help him get up."

Kevin led Lance to Jake and handed him the rope.

"I can't reach the saddle horn to tie it, Jake. Maybe my mom can."

"Hold on, cowboy. You know how to rope. Lasso the saddle horn."

Kevin looked at him in surprise, then his face fell in disappointment. "I can't do it."

"Sure you can. I've watched you. You're the best."

It took Kevin three tries, but he did it. He gave a shout of victory and handed Jake the rest of the rope.

"Excellent roping, cowboy."

"Gee, thanks!" Kevin turned to Beth. "Mom, you put your arms around Jake to help him, and I'll lead Lance. I'll go slow."

Jake winked. "You heard what your son said—put your arms around me."

"Seems like I remember this drill from before," Beth chided. "It's starting to become a habit."

"Ready, Jake?" Kevin shouted.

"Go slow until the rope is tight enough for me to pull it. I can stand myself up. If you go too fast, I'll fall over forward."

"Okay!"

The maneuver worked as planned, and finally Jake was upright. Mud dripped from every part of him.

He looked at Beth, then at Kevin. They were both equally soaked to the skin and muddy, but Jake was by far the worst.

"Beth, why don't you take Kev into the house to get him a hot shower and grab him some dry clothes—take the saddle bag. You get a shower and change, too. My mother has some stuff in the closet. Help yourself, she wouldn't mind. I'll get the horses into the barn and get them settled. How about we all sleep in the cabin for the night? I'll radio our whereabouts to the Gold Buckle when I get in."

Jake scooped up the horses' reins.

"Wait! Wait!" Beth yelled over the storm.

"What?"

"It's Thunder! What happened to his four white socks? He only has two now."

Jake looked at the horse, at Beth, than at Kevin.

"Um…uh…well…" He had just reamed Kevin out for lying, he wasn't about to commit the same crime. "I painted on two more socks with white shoe polish. Looks like it washed off with this rain."

"You did that for me?"

"Well, it seemed to mean a lot to you that your horse had four white socks."

"What's his real name?"

"Sidewinder."

She walked toward Jake and wrapped her arms around his neck. "I love you, Jake Dixon."

"I love you, too, Beth Conroy."

"Yippee!" Kevin jumped up and down, splashing mud and water. "It's about time!"

Beth touched her lips to his and gave him a big hug. In spite of the cold, Jake felt a warm rush. This *had* to be right. It felt right clear down to the toes of his wet socks.

Chapter Fourteen

Jake, Beth and Kevin sat on the plaid sofa in the living room of Em and Dex Dixon's cabin eating popcorn in front of the fire. Their wet, muddy clothes were swirling in the washer. Their soggy shoes were drying near the hearth.

They were all dressed in a mix of clothes from Emily and Dex's closets and dressers and whatever Beth had packed in the saddle bag for Kevin.

They were comfortable together, laughing and chatting. Jake could clearly imagine that they were a family. It was almost as if Beth and Kevin had been sent to him for a reason. Maybe his folks and their contest were just the conduit.

Kevin, sitting between Jake and Beth, was shooting Jake anxious little looks between fistfuls of popcorn. He had peace to make with the youngster. He might as well jump right in.

"Kev, you know, I was way too hard on you in the barn, but I just couldn't figure you out. Still can't. Tell me, why would you stay in a wheelchair when you didn't have to?"

He shrugged as if it were the dumbest question he'd ever heard. "'Cuz of Wheelchair Rodeo."

"What about it?" asked Beth.

"You have to be in a wheelchair to be in WR."

Jake leaned forward on the sofa, his elbows on his knees. "Cowboy, help me out here. What am I missing?"

"Well, you don't have a rodeo for kids who can walk. They can't win your contest. They can't come here and be with you, can't meet the cowboys, can't rope or go on a cool trail ride or ride horses or anything."

"I get it now," Jake said. "You're right. But you still lied, Kev. Faking something is like lying. Right?"

"But when I entered the contest, I couldn't walk."

Beth took Kevin's hand and rested her cheek on his head. "Oh, honey!"

"But, Mom, I wanted to come here really bad. Really bad. And you needed a vacation really bad, too."

"When did you find out you could walk?" Beth asked.

"I had to go to the bathroom one night at home, and I just got up. I was wobbly, but I practiced. I really practiced walking after we won the Gold Buckle contest, so I wasn't really lying when I entered it." His thin smile turned into a frown. "Don't cry, Mom."

"It's a happy cry, sweetie."

Jake noticed that there had been constant tears of happiness in Beth's eyes, and she hadn't been able to let go of Kevin's hand. It was as if she thought that if she let go of his hand, she'd wake up from her dream and find he really couldn't walk.

Kevin turned to Jake. "Do you still like me even though I can walk?" His voice trembled.

"Of course I do!" Jake said, giving the boy a big grin.

"So, are you going to be my father?"

Jake looked at Beth. They had some things to talk about.

"I don't know, Kev. I think that's between your mother and me, but I want you to know one thing. I love you both."

Beth closed her eyes for a moment, then met his gaze. "I was completely wrong about you in the beginning. I still have some unresolved issues, thanks to my late husband's drinking. And when you came to my cabin this morning, I didn't mean..."

Jake waved away her explanation. "I admit, it bothered me. I thought we were past all that." He took a deep breath and let it out. "I did my share of drinking in my younger days, but I'm older and wiser now. I like a beer now and then, but that's all."

Beth nodded. "I think I'll look into counseling for myself on how to handle the whole alcohol issue. Now that Kevin's on the road to recovery, it's time I spent a little energy and effort on me."

"Finally." Jake nodded and smiled encouragingly. "Okay. Now, what else do we have to settle?"

"I promise that I'll never run away again, Jake. I made you get hurt because I ran away, and you had to find me, and then you fell off and couldn't get up, and you probably can't ride because of me."

"Whoa! Slow down." Jake chuckled and put his arm around Kevin's shoulders. "Not true. You shouldn't have run away, but I wasn't paying attention when Lance got spooked. I should have been a better cowboy."

"But, Jake, you're the best."

"Thanks for thinking so."

"But, Kevin, you did take a slot that should have been for another kid," Beth reminded him. "What are you going to do about that? I think we owe the Gold Buckle Ranch to make up for the week."

Jake started to protest, but Beth shot him a "work with me" look.

Kevin shrugged. "I could feed the horses."

"You could," Jake said. "And you can also muck out the stalls."

His face lit up—only a die-hard aspiring cowboy like Kevin would enjoy mucking stalls. Then it dimmed again.

"But we're going home soon, Jake. One day is all I really have left."

He made eye contact with Beth, and her pointed look told him that she was leaving it to him. He'd just as soon forget any kind of punishment for Kev, but he understood where Beth was coming from.

He rubbed his chin. "Well, I think you need to work around the house for your mother through the winter, maybe get an allowance. Then you'll just have to fly back to the Gold Buckle next summer and work off your debt to me. Right?"

"I will, Jake! I will!"

Beth rolled her eyes, but her smile was genuine. Actually, Jake had decided he'd send the plane tickets to them—he wanted to see them—and any money that Kevin earned, Kevin could keep.

Jake saw him stifle a yawn. "I think you're tired. You should head to bed."

"That's right, young man."

"Oh, Mom…"

"Today was a tough day, and tomorrow's going to be really busy," Jake said. "I'm going to need you as my ramrod for Wheelchair Rodeo, okay? You'll be my assistant."

"Wow! Really cool! But what will I tell all the kids?"

"Tell them you're not competing because your last operation finally kicked in. And tell them you worked hard at getting strong, which is true. And then you can tell them that you are going to be mucking stalls until you're twenty years old to give another kid a scholarship here."

"Okay! G'night, Jake."

Kevin held out his hand, and Jake shook it. He felt a warm, happy rush when Kevin's arms curled around his neck in a grateful hug. He'd never get tired of this.

Beth got up with him. Jake heard the murmur of their voices and the door close. Instead of returning to the living room, Beth headed into the kitchen.

Jake knew that he had to have another conversation with Beth, but wasn't particularly looking forward to it. He didn't want to rehash things. He joined her in the kitchen and found her bending over the sink washing the dishes. Suds were clinging to her forearms. Her hair was still wet on the ends.

"Uh-oh, you're thinking again, aren't you. Are you okay?" He put his hands on her shoulders and turned her to face him.

"When you said you loved me, did you mean it?"

"I did."

She took a deep breath. "Well, I meant it, too."

Love should be happy, but there was sadness in the air. Jake's heart sat like a lump in his chest. He couldn't have her or Kevin. He was a bull rider. That's what he had to do.

She turned around. A solitary tear ran down her face, and he wiped it off with his thumb.

"What is it?" he asked.

"I don't think I'm ever going to understand Kevin—or you. You were wonderful with him." She gazed into his eyes. "And I'd like to thank you for apologizing to him."

"I didn't handle things with Kev the way I should have back in the barn."

She held up a soapy hand. "You apologized. I would have reacted the same way in your situation. Remember, I didn't handle things the way I should have when I first met *you.* I realize now that you're not addicted to alcohol. You're addicted to titles and records and being on top." She closed her eyes as if building up strength, then opened them. "I know you don't like being compared to Brad, but you're like him in one regard."

"What's that?"

"He never thought about Kevin or me." She took a deep breath. "Remember when Kevin asked you if you still love him now that he can walk?"

He nodded.

"Well, I'll still love you when you can't. I know that risk-taking is part of you. You live for the challenge, the man-against-beast thing, for more titles. No guts, no glory. Whatever." She hesitated, fishing for words.

"Go ahead. I hear a 'but' coming."

"*But* I need to be with someone who thinks about us. If you were in a car crash, it'd be different. I'd take care of you. But if you died under Twister or another bull?" She shook her head. "I don't think I could handle it."

"You don't have much faith in my riding, Beth. Just because I have a couple of minor injuries—"

"Minor injuries?" She took a deep breath and let it out. "Let me remind you that you had to be pulled up from the ground by a horse, Jake. Not once, but two or three times. Who's going to pick you up from the arena floor when you get bucked off next time? Even if you weren't bucked off and jumped off, would you land on your feet? Could you run away?"

He remembered thinking the same thing when he was lying on his back in the mud. "I'm hoping my adrenaline would keep me going."

"You'll need more than adrenaline, cowboy. You'll need a forklift."

He chuckled. "Remember, Clint Scully is the best in the business."

"Well, no matter what you call Clint, you're also putting him at risk. You're not in top form."

He held his hands up. Damn, how could he argue with anything she was saying? She was right, and he knew it.

"Okay. I know where you stand. I get it."

"And?"

"And I'm going to ride tomorrow."

She concentrated on the dishes again. Then she lifted her head and smiled sadly at him. "Okay. Kevin and I will be there. But if you go down, you won't see me anymore. I can't watch another person that I love get hurt."

He gathered her in his arms and hung on tight. "Will you at least cheer for me?"

"Of course I will, and you know Kevin will." She held his face in the palms of her hands. "Be safe, Jake."

"I'll try." He kissed her with all the love he had in his heart for her. He wished things could be different, but for now, he had to think of Wheelchair Rodeo—and not himself. If he rode that bounty bull, WR would be set financially for a long time.

Kevin's confession had the ideas rolling around in his head. With the money, he could expand to include kids who weren't disabled. Or even kids in need of psychiatric care. He'd talk to Trot's child psychologist pal, and get him to commit to some volunteer hours next year. He could even include kids who were starting to get into trouble, criminal trouble. He'd let them work off their anger by pitching in at the ranch.

There were all sorts of things he could do with Harvey Trumble's money.

She walked over to kiss him good-night. "I want you to know that I've had a wonderful time at the Gold Buckle this week. You're doing good things here."

"This sounds like goodbye."

"It is."

He fisted his hands in her hair and feasted on her lips. He wanted to be with her tonight, to make love with her one last time. He wanted to hold her in his arms all night, and wake up next to her in the morning. That wouldn't happen—not with Kevin in the room next door.

It was better they part like this anyway.

"Good night, Beth."

"Good night, Jake."

Minutes later, stretched out on the couch, he thought that he hadn't felt this bad since he had to put his first horse down. The day after tomorrow, he'd be saying goodbye to two people he loved with all his heart.

The next day dawned sunny and breezy. They rode back to the Gold Buckle in time for breakfast. Beth rode alone. Jake shared Lance with Kevin.

It was a party atmosphere when they returned. Kids gathered around Kevin. Beth heard him say, "My last operation finally kicked in and I've been practicing walking. Being in WR made me stronger."

Jake walked over to the group. "And Kevin here rescued me. I got thrown by Lance and couldn't get up. Kevin did some fancy roping of the saddle horn, and I was able to pull myself up."

"Way cool."

"Awesome."

"Totally radical, Kev."

Kevin's eyes met Jake's and Jake saw that the boy was getting uncomfortable with the attention, so he changed the subject. "Kevin's withdrawn from the competition, and he's going to be my ramrod for Wheelchair Rodeo tonight at the arena. Is everyone ready?"

"Yeah!" yelled the kids.

"I can't hear you," Jake said.

"YEAH!"

Jake's fist pumped the air. "All right!"

It was finally time for Wheelchair Rodeo. Beth sat in the stands at the Mountain Springs Arena, content to watch Kevin fetch and carry for Jake. It definitely was a miracle watching him walk after two long years in a wheelchair. He was still stiff, sometimes awkward, but when he was tired, he sat down.

She had felt euphoric when she first saw Kevin walk. But the euphoria had faded somewhat when she realized that Jake might soon be in a chair himself.

The stands were fairly crowded. The word had gone out on radio and TV that WR had been rained out the previous day and was scheduled to take place before the main event.

Also before the main event, Jake Dixon was scheduled to ride Twister.

"Twister," the announcer said, "has successfully thrown off thirty-five previous riders. The bounty on him is $150,000. The *Wyoming Journal* is also putting up some nice money. All money will go to Wheelchair Rodeo, the special program run by Jake Dixon and his folks out at the Gold Buckle Ranch right here in Mountain Springs."

"I hope Harvey Trumble eats crow," Beth heard K.C. tell Ramon. "If anyone can ride that bull, Jake can."

"He's not in top form," Ramon replied. "I don't think he has a chance. Jake had him twice before and was bucked off both times."

Beth closed her eyes and said another prayer for

Jake. How could the man be so stupid? Then she saw him down there with the kids and she knew he'd do anything for them.

She could almost understand him—after all, she'd do anything for Kevin. She took a deep breath and thought positive thoughts. Things had to work out okay.

During the competition Beth cheered for all the WR participants. Jake saw to it that all the kids got some kind of mention and accolades. They were beaming and so were their parents.

When it came time for the trophy and ribbon presentations for Wheelchair Rodeo, Kevin handed the awards to Jake as they were presented, until there was nothing left on the table.

"I have a special award to pass out today," Jake announced to the crowd. "It's for a special cowboy who used his roping skills that he learned during Wheelchair Rodeo to help out another cowboy in need. Kevin Conroy, will you come over here, please?"

Kevin's eyes were round with surprise. He hurried over and stood by Jake.

"Ladies and gentlemen," said Jake, "I was the cowboy that Kevin helped."

Jake waited for the applause to stop, but the cowboys and the kids wouldn't stop clapping. Jake stepped back for Kevin to be the focus. Kevin grinned from ear to ear. Finally Jake held up his hands and the applause began to die down.

"I'd like to present this special award to Kevin Conroy." He held up a huge gold belt buckle. "I hope you don't mind, Kevin. It's a little used. It's the gold buckle I won at the PBR Finals a couple of years ago."

Kevin held up the buckle for the audience to see. The applause was hearty. Lights flashed. Beth wished she had a camera, but Emily was front and center with her own. She'd ask for duplicates from her.

Jake squatted down and, without hesitation, Kevin hugged him. Beth let her tears flow. It was a beautiful moment in her life, a moment to be treasured.

She hoped that Jake would make the time to keep in touch with Kevin, and she'd let Kevin call Jake as much as he wanted. She'd certainly like to keep in touch with Jake herself and to see how he was doing. She was going to miss him terribly.

As Jake and Kevin shook hands, she swallowed hard against the lump of sadness in her throat. There was no way around it. She had to return home tomorrow and get back to work, get back to her life. She had bills yet to pay. With continued hydrotherapy, Kevin would become even stronger.

But there was no denying that when she stepped on that plane, and they closed and locked the cabin door, she'd be in total agony.

She tried to relax, tried to shake out the tension in her muscles. Even more terrible than getting on that plane tomorrow was doing what she had to do now: watch Jake ride Twister.

The volunteers and the cowboys got the kids settled into the stands. Kevin appeared and sat next to her, showing her his Gold Buckle. "It's awesome, Mom."

She traced Jake's name on the buckle, which was probably worth several thousand dollars to rodeo collectors, but it held more value than that for Kevin. His hero had given it to him.

And his hero had turned out to be worthy of Kevin's admiration.

She put her arm around her son's shoulders and hugged him to her. "That's a great reward for a great job."

"Mom?"

"Yes?

"Do we *have* to go tomorrow? Really? Can't we stay here?"

She took a deep breath. "I'm sorry, Kev, but that's where we live. That's where my job is."

"But I thought you *liked* Jake?"

"I do, honey, but Jake has his own life. Our week is over here."

How could she tell him that Jake had chosen his bull riding over them? That he might end up severely injured after this ride, or the next, or the next?

Kevin bent his head to stare at the buckle, and Beth knew that his little heart was breaking as much as hers.

Much to her surprise, Harvey Trumble took a seat next to her. He was with a good-looking man in his mid-twenties with his arm in a cast. Beth assumed that it was Keith, the man who had accused Jake of breaking his arm.

"Hello, Mr. Trumble."

He looked at her suspiciously. "Do I know you from somewhere?"

"A couple of days ago. The Last Chance Saloon. I was with Jake Dixon."

One side of his lip curled up. "Oh, yeah."

"This is my son, Kevin. Kevin Conroy."

Kevin leaned across her to shake hands with Mr.

Trumble. Trumble seemed surprised, but he took Kevin's hand. Harvey pointed a thumb toward the man next to him.

"This is my son, Keith."

Keith waved but didn't extend his hand.

Kevin waved back. "Hi."

"Hello," Beth said.

"Whatcha got there, boy?" Mr. Trumble asked Kevin.

"Kevin was awarded a Gold Buckle from Jake for helping him when he needed it," Beth said.

Harvey seemed to lighten up when Kevin showed him his buckle. "What good deed did you do?"

"I roped a saddle horn so Jake could hold on to it and get up from the mud."

"Why couldn't he get up from the mud?"

"Because he has too many injuries. He needs some operations," Kevin told the man. "Dr. Trotter told him to quit, but Jake said that he has to ride Twister to give the money to Wheelchair Rodeo."

Puzzled, Beth looked at Kevin. "How do you know all this?"

He shrugged. "I heard Jake tell Dr. Trotter."

Trumble cleared his throat and shifted in his seat.

"His sponsors are dropping him due in part to you, no doubt." Beth shook her head. "How could you hate him so much? No matter what happens to him, he's going to do it for Wheelchair Rodeo. Do you get that, Mr. Trumble? Jake could end up in a wheelchair himself, and he knows that. But you know what makes him a hero? He's not doing it for himself. Not this time. He's doing it for the kids."

"You tell him, Mom!" Kevin said.

"Geez, Pop, I didn't know Jake was hurt that much," Keith said.

Harvey turned toward Keith. "Didn't you tell me that Jake said you weren't good enough for his sister?"

"That's what he said."

"Mr. Trumble, Jake told me that *no one* was good enough for his sister and that Keith continued to put his hands on her *after* she told him to stop." Beth looked pointedly at Keith. "What would you do if you were Jake and Karen was your sister?"

Harvey stood and motioned with his hand. "We need to talk, Keith. Let's go."

He watched his son walk down the bleachers, then he turned to Beth and tweaked his hat. "The money is Jake's whether he rides the bull or not, but I'm going to try to stop him from riding."

But it was too late. The announcer was pumping up the crowd for Jake's ride. Beth looked over at the chutes and could see only the top of Jake's black hat. His bull rope was vertical in the air and she knew he was working rosin into it to make it sticky. Then he'd wrap the bull rope around his riding hand.

A huge screen hanging from the roof of the arena showed a close-up of him, and she could see him concentrating on his wrap.

"Be careful, Jake. Please be careful," she prayed.

"Go, Jake! You can ride that old bull!" yelled Kevin.

Beth held her breath.

The chute gate opened. Twister sprang out into the arena and began to spin. He was all muscle, yet surprisingly agile for his nineteen hundred pounds. Snot poured out of his nose in ribbons when he bucked, and true-to-his name he twisted in midair, trying to shake Jake off his back. Jake drifted left, then centered himself—a remarkable feat.

"Hang on, Jake. Hang on!" Beth screamed. Her nails dug into her palms as she watched the bull spin left.

"You got 'em, Jake!"

The spectators were going wild. The clock showed three seconds. It was the longest three seconds of her life.

Twister reversed the spin. Jake stayed with him, but he was barely hanging on. Then he was over to the side.

"Five seconds!" Kevin screamed. "Hold on, Jake!"

Beth sprang to her feet. "Do it, Jake! Do it!"

Six seconds.

The bull reversed again. Jake was hanging dangerously over the side of the bull. With every jump, the animal's hooves moved closer to his face.

It wasn't pretty, but he was still in the game.

Seven seconds. Eight seconds!

The buzzer rang. Jake let go, but with the bull still spinning Jake was tossed off like a rag doll. He lay on the ground, unmoving.

"Get up, Jake. Get up!" Beth shouted.

He didn't. He couldn't.

Her heart sank.

He's a good man. Don't let him be hurt. Don't let him be paralyzed.

Clint Scully and two other bullfighters managed to get the bull out of the arena as a team of paramedics helped Jake up. Jake punched the air and flung his hat across the arena. Then the audience was on its feet, going wild.

Beth and Kevin high-fived one another and hugged.

On the big screen, Beth saw the whiteness around Jake's mouth, a sign of pain that probably only she noticed. But, thank heaven, he was alive and walking and didn't seem any worse.

She watched as Jake slowly made his way in front of the bleachers where they were sitting. Standing in the arena, he waved to them. Clint Scully came up behind Jake and plopped his hat back on his head, and the two exchanged kidding punches.

Beth's throat was raw from screaming. She blew him a kiss. Jake laughed.

"Yeah, Jake!" Kevin yelled.

Jake punched the air again. Kevin did the same in return. Then he walked off for the check presentation. This check would be for one hundred and fifty thousand dollars—from the stock contractor who owned Twister.

Beth settled back in her chair as she watched him accept the check. Then the announcer had the audience do a countdown as to when the Challenge would go live on TV.

The Jake Dixon Bull Riders Challenge was starting.

Every rider was introduced and stood in the middle of the arena. After the last introduction, geysers of glittering fireworks sprouted up from the arena floor.

Jake's name was announced, and when he walked out, she and Kevin yelled at the top of their lungs.

Everyone stood for the National Anthem and for a new Cowboy/Cowgirl Prayer written and read by Dex Dixon.

When the applause ended, Jake stood in the middle of the dark arena, a spotlight focused on him.

His deep voice vibrated through Beth's bones.

"Ladies and gentleman, honored guests of Wheelchair Rodeo, and all you professional bull riders who have joined us today, my name is Jake Dixon and on behalf of my parents, Emily and Dex Dixon, we'd like to welcome you to the Third Annual Jake Dixon Gold Buckle Ranch Bull Riders Challenge."

There was a roar of applause. Jake waited.

"We've had some excitement here today, haven't we?"

The applause and cheering was deafening. Beth and Kevin added their own encouragement to the noise.

"And there's more excitement to come. So everyone...get ready to rock!" Music blared as the lights went on in the arena. Jake waved his hat in the air as the announcer took over.

Kevin pointed to something in the program, and Beth leaned over to see what he was indicating. Before she knew what was happening, she heard whistles and clapping from the spectators around her and Jake slipped into the seat next to her, the seat that Harvey Trumble had just vacated. Those around them in the stands were slapping Jake on the back and shaking his hand.

"Congratulations!" Beth said.

"Cool, Jake!"

"Thanks." He grinned and took Beth's hand in his.

"Are you okay?" Beth asked.

"Never better," he replied. "But listen to the announcer."

The announcer's voice echoed through the arena. "Jake Dixon has withdrawn from today's competition. He told me that he has to tell a certain lady that a gold ring is better than a Gold Buckle. What do you think that means, folks?"

Jake struggled to get down on one knee, using the chairs on both sides of him as leverage.

"What are you doing, Jake?" Kevin asked.

Jake let out a long breath. "I'm trying to propose to your mother. Okay with you, Kevin?"

"Cool!"

Beth tried to swallow, but the lump in her throat wouldn't let her.

Jake kissed the back of her hand. "Beth Conroy, will you marry me?"

Beth finally found her voice. "But...your career."

"How much more on top could I be? I have you and Kevin. I don't need anything else. Okay, maybe a couple more little cowboys or cowgirls. Is that all right with you?"

She laughed, tears in her eyes. "Perfectly all right."

"And maybe I'd like to teach bull riding and horseback riding, expand the Gold Buckle programs, maybe go back to school, build a small hotel on the ranch, build us a home..." He stopped to take a breath. "I'll need your help and Kevin's. That okay with you?"

"Absolutely! But what about your surgery?"

"I'll let Trot know he can crack me open as soon as possible and fix me up."

She dried her cheeks with a swipe of her hand. "I'm so glad."

"Well, will you marry this broken-down cowboy?"

"Honey, if you don't marry him, I will!" said a lady two rows up. Everyone laughed.

"Sorry. He's mine. All mine," she shot over her shoulder, then turned to Jake. "I'd love to marry you!" Beth bent over to kiss him.

He pulled her close and they sealed their promise with a kiss.

"Oh brother," Kevin said. "Ick."

Laughter broke them apart. As Jake tried to stand, several people came to his assistance.

He gathered Beth in his arms, and looked down at Kevin. "Are you sure that it's okay with you, cowboy?"

"Do I get to keep Killer? Are Emily and Dex going to be my grandparents? Can I be a ranch hand? Can I help you with Wheelchair Rodeo?"

"Yes. To all of it." Jake held out his hand.

"Okay with me." Kevin slipped his Gold Buckle into his pocket and shook Jake's hand. Then he hopped up on a chair, put his arms around the both of them as far as he could stretch and hugged as hard as he could.

As thirteen thousand people watched them on the huge monitors in the Mountain Springs Arena and another ten million or so watched on TV, Jake and Beth kissed.

* * * * *

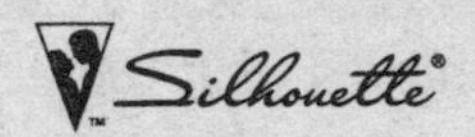
Silhouette®

DESERT
ROGUES

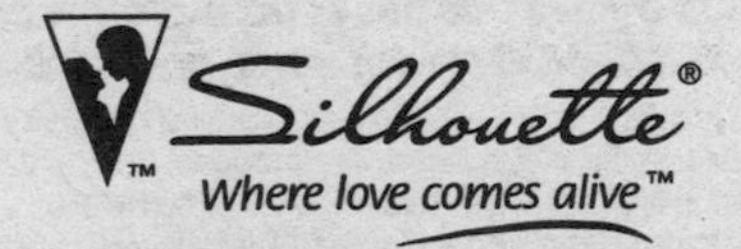
Silhouette®
Where love comes alive™